Joan Aiken and The Murder Room

››› This title is part of The Murder Room, our series dedicated to making available out-of-print or hard-to-find titles by classic crime writers.

Crime fiction has always held up a mirror to society. The Victorians were fascinated by sensational murder and the emerging science of detection; now we are obsessed with the forensic detail of violent death. And no other genre has so captivated and enthralled readers.

Vast troves of classic crime writing have for a long time been unavailable to all but the most dedicated frequenters of second-hand bookshops. The advent of digital publishing means that we are now able to bring you the backlists of a huge range of titles by classic and contemporary crime writers, some of which have been out of print for decades.

From the genteel amateur private eyes of the Golden Age and the femmes fatales of pulp fiction, to the morally ambiguous hard-boiled detectives of mid twentieth-century America and their descendants who walk our twenty-first century streets, The Murder Room has it all. ›››

The Murder Room
Where Criminal Minds Meet

themurderroom.com

Acclaim for Joan Aiken

THE SILENCE OF HERONDALE
'A first thriller which has the unmistakeable whiff of success' *Telegraph*
'Don't miss . . . guaranteed unputdownable' *Observer*

TROUBLE WITH PRODUCT X
'Witty and acute . . . a nice romantic thriller' *Punch*
'Bubbling and engaging story' *Telegraph*

HATE BEGINS AT HOME
'Contemporary Gothic, executed with fine melodramatic conviction' *Financial Times*
'Terrifyingly enclosed spine-chiller' *Sunday Telegraph*
'An essay in sheer terror' *Birmingham Evening Mail*

THE RIBS OF DEATH
'Excellent characterisation, especially of the likeable heroine narrator' *Sunday Telegraph*
'A fast, lively story that builds to a fiery denouement' *Daily Telegraph*
'Unusual, enthralling, full of wry fun' *Sunday Times*

DIED ON A RAINY SUNDAY
'Joan Aiken has established herself as one of the leading purveyors of suspense' *Guardian*

Joan Aiken (1924–2004)

Joan Aiken, English-born daughter of American poet Conrad Aiken, began her writing career in the 1950s. Working for *Argosy* magazine as a copy editor but also as the anonymous author of articles and stories to fill up their pages, she was adept at inventing a wealth of characters and fantastic situations, and went on to produce hundreds of stories for *Good Housekeeping, Vogue, Vanity Fair* and many other magazines. Some of those early stories became novels, such as *The Silence of Herondale*, first published fifty years ago in 1964.

Although her first agent famously told her to stick to short stories, saying she would never be able to sustain a full-length novel, Joan Aiken went on to win the *Guardian* Children's Fiction Prize for *The Whispering Mountain*, and the Edgar Alan Poe award for her adult novel *Night Fall.* Her best known children's novel, *The Wolves of Willoughby Chase*, was acclaimed by *Time* magazine as 'a genuine small masterpiece'.

In 1999 she was awarded an MBE for her services to children's literature, and although best known as a children's writer, Joan Aiken wrote many adult novels, both modern and historical, with her trademark wit and verve. Many have a similar gothic flavour to her children's writing, and were much admired by readers and critics alike. As she said 'The only difference I can see is that children's books have happier endings than those for adults.' You have been warned . . .

By Joan Aiken

(Select bibliography of titles published in The Murder Room)

The Silence of Herondale (1964)
The Fortune Hunters (1965)
Trouble With Product X (1966)
Hate Begins at Home (1967)
The Ribs of Death (1967)
Died on a Rainy Sunday (1972)

The Fortune Hunters

Joan Aiken

An Orion book

This edition published by
The Orion Publishing Group Ltd
Orion House
5 Upper St Martin's Lane
London WC2H 9EA

An Hachette UK company
A CIP catalogue record for this book is available from the British Library

ISBN 978 1 4719 1671 7

www.orionbooks.co.uk

Introduction

As well as writing children's books, beloved by generations and still avidly read today, Joan Aiken also quickly established herself in the 1960s as a witty author of adult suspense with the ability to keep readers of all ages on the edge of their seats. Too inventive to stick with a formula she nevertheless revelled in the atmosphere of Gothic parody and was often compared with Mary Stewart. In the tradition of Jane Austen's *Northanger Abbey* Joan gave her long-suffering heroines a set of literary references to support them through their frightful ordeals, and usually a quirky sense of humour, making full use of her own extensive literary background.

In true Gothic style these hapless heroines would become embroiled in a series of events not of their own making, and were usually possessed of many stalwart characteristics – not least a literary education – if not always endowed with obvious physical charms. And they were, of course, always a version of Joan herself: small, slightly gap toothed, and red haired, extremely enterprising, physically intrepid and fearless to the end. She loved to share episodes from her own life, and those who knew her also became accustomed to the dubious pleasure of discovering (albeit disguised) episodes from their own lives in her books – although told with such warmth and humour that she was swiftly forgiven!

What she could also guarantee were indefatigably sinister villains, mounting and finely controlled tension, complex plots, and hair-raising climaxes, often with an unusually high body count. As she confessed, 'I often have more characters than I know what to do with.'

Admired and enjoyed by many of her crime-writing contemporaries such as John Creasey, H.R.F. Keating, Francis Iles and Edmund Crispin, Joan Aiken's adult novels of suspense have lost none of their charm, and their period settings are sure to appeal to a new generation of readers who grew up on her children's books.

Lizza Aiken, October 2014

I

It was wonderful and miserable—wonderful to be driving home to her own house in the green-gold late autumn evening; miserable because there was nobody to share it with. Wonderful to be able to sink into bed without setting the alarm, chilling to think of Joanna's sidelong smile—"Of course I know you *say* you'll be coming back to the office in a month or two, but after all there's no need to, is there?" Wonderful Joanna, false, dear friend, such fun to be with, such a diverting, barbed line of wit about office colleagues —and undoubtedly, in different company, about oneself. Wonderful Joanna, who happened to know about this enchanting miniature house for sale situated a safe, oblivious distance from London; wonderful Joanna who perhaps wanted one's job for herself?

The little car sped on across the marsh through the green-gold light towards a bank of black cloud.

"Why such a little car?" Joanna had said. "If it were I, I'd splash on something really ostentatious. But of course you'd despise that, wouldn't you? Always such good taste. . . ."

It was queer how the money cut you off from your friends. Whether you spent it or saved it, you couldn't be right; you were ostentatious and patronising if you bought them all drinks and mohair sweaters, mean if you didn't. And so many of them just avoiding you, as if money were an infectious disease, rather an unpleasant one. The sensitive stinkers, thought Annette, swerving to avoid a leisurely hare tittupping across the road; *I* wouldn't value my own nice feelings above somebody else's loneliness.

Of course it was a classic situation. There was no need

to feel herself peculiarly ill-used. The Sunday papers each week were dotted with heart-rending human-interest stories of pools winners who started hitting the bottle and skidded to the verge of suicide because their erstwhile friends and neighbours self-consciously shunned them. Sudden wealth was the great insulator, second only to sudden bereavement. And she, Annette, had the bad luck to be afflicted with both. Money oppressed people, grief scared them—made them feel, she supposed, inadequate. (But who wants adequacy when he is unhappy? You don't ask people to dart about and be efficient—what you desperately long for is the warmth of casual human companionship.)

It was interesting, too, Annette mused, swooping the car over one of the recurrent little bridges that spanned the crisscross marsh dykes: the people who normally seem most confident, most capable, are the first to buckle and turn tail in the face of someone else's unhappiness. Because, fundamentally, it is their own performance they are worried about, not the other person's needs? You have to have humility to be able to help people in trouble.

Take Philip, for example.

Let's not take Philip, her mind objected.

Oh, very well. I was only pointing out—

Well, don't. And anyway, Philip *has* humility—as well as a kind heart. He is really very diffident about himself.

Diffident for the wrong reason: from self-consciousness.

Oh, be quiet! And tend to your driving.

Switching her mind from this unsatisfactory—and all too familiar—interior dialogue, she closed her right-hand window, on which rain was beginning to splat, and concentrated firmly on the road ahead.

I'm glad I'm not walking, she thought with a wonderful feeling of luxury. At the end of this bleak, rain-swept road her house waited for her, snug and firelit.

No boring tasks demanded her attention, or uncongenial people: there were no awkward interviews to be faced, obligations of telling artists how their work had failed to achieve what was wanted, or efforts to reconcile antagonistic viewpoints in temperamental office colleagues. None of that. And no worries about late contributions, irate printers, copyright infringements, disputes over fees, libellous errors in captions. No cares of any kind. Just the little house ready to welcome her, filled with the furniture she had lovingly sought and bought, gay with the colour-schemes she had chosen. I really am extraordinarily lucky, Annette told herself.

Then she saw the woman with the push-chair.

The rain was flailing down by now, bouncing up from the road in gravelly splashes, but the woman, clad only in a shapeless grey costume, with no topcoat, walked slowly in the downpour, doggedly, as if she had a long way to go and felt there would be no point in hurrying. Who was in the push-chair Annette couldn't see—an adult evidently from the size, but so muffled up in rugs and waterproof sheeting that no face was visible.

Braking, she drew to a halt beside the pair, shoved down the window, and shouted, "Want a lift?"

As if they wouldn't! However, the woman took her time about answering. She had a prim, down-drawn face, hardly raised her lashless eyes to Annette's but kept them fixed mostly on the tips of her sodden laced shoes.

"Well—it's kind of you, but hardly worth it now—we're so wet already—"

"Oh nonsense," Annette said. "You must have miles to go. There's not a house along this road till Crowbridge. Is that where you're going?"

"Yes, but the push-chair—you could never take it in the car."

"It folds, doesn't it? It'll go in the trunk," Annette said with immense optimism.

"And then you'll get so wet and we'll muddy your car—"

The woman seemed prepared to stand arguing forever with the rain flattening her grey hair, but Annette jumped out decisively, hugging her red corduroy coat round her, and opened the trunk and a rear door.

"Now," she said, "if you can help your—" Was the occupant of the chair male or female? She still hadn't seen the face, which was hooded over by a fold of groundsheet. The woman, however, having apparently come to a decision at last, edged the muffled figure into the back seat with surprising speed and then helped Annette fold the big push-chair, tipping it sideways into the opened trunk and tethering it to the spare tyre with a bit of rope.

"The lid won't quite shut; never mind. It won't fall out. Jump in quick!"

They were off again with a spurt of muddy water from the wheels, cutting through the puddles on the ill-kept road.

The woman had elected to go in the back seat by her charge. She evidently preferred not to talk, and after a few commonplaces about the suddenness of the storm Annette abandoned any attempt at conversation. In any case she needed most of her concentration for the road, dimly seen through the weaving ripple of rain on the windscreen.

Not a word, meantime, from the second passenger.

But presently Annette heard a low, harsh humming, all on two notes, from behind her. At first she thought it was some trick of the rain on the roof, then the woman said, "Don't, Doris," and the humming stopped.

So the other passenger was a female. What was the matter with her?

"You live in Crowbridge?" Annette said presently, feeling the silence grow oppressive.

"Yes. If you could put us down just this side of the town—before you get to the Sea Gate . . ."

The toneless voice wavered and halted; suddenly Annette realised that the woman's evident reluctance to talk came not from lack of manners or hostility but from desperate nervousness. Why? Was Annette giving a lift to a case of bubonic?

Although she had put this suggestion to herself as a joke, somehow it stuck in Annette's mind, and, like most highly strung people in the near presence of illness, she began to feel odd symptoms—her scalp prickled, her shoulder blades ached.

"You're an ass," she told herself. "Finish convalescing

from one illness before you start imagining yourself into another."

Just the same, her neck did tickle. . . . She rubbed it. A moment later she rubbed it again.

"Don't, Doris," said the woman in the back.

Don't what? Annette wondered. The humming had not begun again.

The road looped up, here, over a shoulder of high land; ahead lay another grey, drenched expanse of marsh, with Crowbridge, the little town perched on its knoll, barely visible in the distance.

"You would have had about four and a half miles to walk," Annette said. "You would have been soaked."

"It's not far when you're used to it."

Annette rubbed her neck again.

"Doris!" the woman said sharply.

There was a queer, hoarse murmur. Then, for a moment of incredulous horror, Annette felt two hands which came over the back of her seat and rubbed lovingly, sensuously, on her throat—for a moment only, before they suddenly clamped on her windpipe in a fierce, throttling grip. A hoarse voice was whispering in her ear: *"Now I've got you. I've waited a long time for this. Now I've got you. I've waited a long time for this. Now I've got you. I've waited—"*

Over and over, like a parrot, or a faulty record.

Annette gasped, jerking sideways—and then mercifully got her foot on the brake and kept it jammed there as the car reeled across the road and came to rest against the opposite bank.

"Doris! Let go of the lady's neck! At once, I tell you!"

There was a guttural murmured protest and the sound of a smack. The grip abruptly relaxed. Annette leaned forward, gagging and coughing.

"Are—are you all right?" The woman was really desperate now. "I'm not—I should never have accepted—"

"I'll be all right in a minute," Annette coughed. Why didn't you warn me? she wanted to say.

"We'll get out here and walk the rest of the way—if

you wouldn't mind helping me down with the push-chair—I can't manage it on my own. I'm ever so sorry, I really am. I should never have let you—"

"You should never have let *her*."

Annette got out, and the rain steadied her—that and not being within reach of those bony, garrotting hands. "What's the matter with her?"

"She's—she's gentle as a rule." The woman made a fumbling, helpless attempt to undo the rope that tethered the push-chair in the trunk. Annette helped her speechlessly and then stood in fascinated repugnance while Doris was shoe-horned out of the car.

Doris was reluctant to move—but in the end she came, voicing her protest in a low-pitched mumble that continued all the time she was being strapped and groundsheeted. This time Annette did get a view of her. A big, strong girl, Doris, her hair lank, her face, with its sideways drag, lost, forlorn, wild . . . but with a flicker of malice at the back of the deepset, unfocused eyes. A face to give one the cold grue.

"I'm ever so grateful to you," the woman said, tucking a last fold of the waterproof sheet carefully over her charge. "Ever so sorry. I do hope you'll be all right." She went on nervously, her knuckles white as they gripped the handle of the chair, "I'd be very obliged if—if you wouldn't mention what happened to anyone."

"No, all right. I'll be fine, thanks," Annette said dryly. "You're sure *you're* okay with her?" But, without waiting to answer, the woman had tucked her head down and scuttled off into the rainy twilight towards Crowbridge.

Well! Annette climbed back into the car, absently massaging her bruised throat. She didn't, somehow, relish the thought of passing the couple on their plodding way, and decided to give them time to get into the town before starting the car again. It couldn't be more than fifteen minutes' walk for them from here.

She switched on the parking lights, pulled the car over to the correct side of the road, and leaned back in her seat, lighting a cigarette with hands that shook slightly.

Did the town contain a home for mental defectives? It was recommended as a salubrious resort for retired people and convalescents, with its peace, its seclusion, its sea air, its nine-hole golf course; perfect for patients recovering from heart strain, ulcers, or the stress of city life; but Annette couldn't remember any mention of an asylum. . . .

She had smoked her cigarette to its end and was sitting in a half-doze, reluctant to move, when somebody tapped on the window a couple of inches from her right cheek. Annette started violently and then, angry at herself for this betrayal of nerviness, opened the window.

"I beg your pardon if I disturbed your train of thought, but are you going to park here for the night, or are you going into Crowbridge?"

A cheerful, bearded giant was framed in the window, looking down at her. On a closer view of her face he gave a small, startled whistle of dismay.

"I say, are you feeling queer or something? Are you all right?"

"Of course I'm all right," Annette said curtly. "Sorry—I didn't mean to snap at you"—seeing his expression of concern intensify if anything. "It's only that I'm convalescing after jaundice and I have dizzy spells occasionally; but they don't last any time. What can I do for you—do you want a lift into Crowbridge?"

"Yes," he said unabashedly. "I'm parked a hundred yards back with two flat tyres—the site where I'm working is death on 'em. I've got a dinner date tonight at eight, otherwise I wouldn't object to hoofing it. But are you sure you're okay to drive? I'll take her in for you if you're feeling faint."

"No, really I'm all right now. I shan't send you into the ditch. Hop in."

He was so large that he had to bend into three before he could negotiate her front seat. His windbreaker and corduroys were soaking wet and plastered with mud.

"What a climate!" he said. "But one has to put up with it. They don't have Roman remains where I come from—or none that have been discovered yet."

"Where do you come from?"

"New Zealand. I'm over here on an archaeological fellowship."

"Oh. When you said you were working on a site, I took it for granted you were a bricklayer."

"Bricklayers don't work such long hours," he said, grinning.

Arrived at the town, they ran in under the massive fourteenth-century Sea Gate and nosed through narrow, rainswept, empty streets.

"Where can I drop you?"

Crowbridge at night—even on a wet, windy October night—looked like pure magic. Small street-lamps, tethered high on the timbered sides of houses, threw glancing diagonal patches of light down cobbled sidewalks.

"Isn't it a witch-town?" he said. "I'm staying at the Bell. Is that out of your way? Do you live here?"

"No, it's not out of my way. I have a house in Crossbow Lane, round a couple of corners farther on."

"I really am grateful," he said when she stopped outside the Bell Inn with its wildly swinging signboard. "Can we meet again? I'd like to buy you a drink sometime in return for that ride. My name's Noel Hanaker."

"Annette Sheldon," she said. "I'd like that very much. Hadn't you better hurry now if your date's at eight?"

"Too right," he said cheerfully. "If it was a girl it wouldn't matter—many's the sultry blonde I've kept waiting; they lap it up—but it's an artistic old cove that I've got a letter of introduction to—famous type, name of Crispin James. Wouldn't do to keep him hanging about. Good night, Miss Sheldon—it is Miss, isn't it?"

"Yes, it's Miss," she said.

"—and thanks again."

Annette released the handbrake and eased her car gently on over the cobbles. Crispin James! she thought. Well, well! How in the world did that rugged young extrovert come to be acquainted with such an internationally famous figure? If there was anything that outran the renown of Crispin James's paintings, it was his reputation for exclusiveness, for inaccessibility, except among the equally great. Playing chess with Hemingway, sipping ouzo with the king of Greece, perching on a crag with the Dalai Lama, perhaps, but dinner at the Bell with an obscure young archaeologist from New Zealand, she would have thought, emphatically no. Maybe his reputation belied him, though; maybe he was more democratic than the glossy magazines made out.

She drove on round the tortuous, tiny town to Crossbow Lane and parked the car at the kerb.

One of the streep-lamps was attached to her own timbered cottage, and its light showed a length of rope dangling out of the car luggage compartment.

That's odd, she thought. I wonder how it got pulled out?

She opened the trunk and found the other end of the rope attached to the spare tyre. How peculiar. Who had bothered to do that? Someone at the garage while they were servicing the car? But what for? And the inside of the trunk was damp as if it had been open in the rain. But there had been no rain all day, until after she had started the drive home from the furniture sale at Long Green. Had she been driving with the lid open?

Annette stood with her fingers pressed tightly to her forehead for a moment, staring at the empty trunk, at the trailing rope. Then, with a small, despairing shake of her head she shut and locked the car.

Rest and warmth, that was what she needed, and a hot drink—then perhaps she would remember the origin of the rope.

There was no light on in the front room but through the window she could see the reflection of flames dancing on the ceiling. It was Mrs Fairhall's evening off, but she had lit the fires, bless her. And would have left something for supper. How easy it was, Annette reflected, to get used to other people's services. Up till six months ago she had been proud of the fact that nobody else had ever so much as boiled an egg for her—and now here she was, a bloated plutocrat, employing labour right and left.

She fitted her key into the lock and then, glancing up,

noticed a light in the guest-room window. Heavens, of course it was Friday, and Joanna had arrived for the weekend. Would her feelings be hurt because Annette hadn't been there to receive her?

"Hallo-oo, is that you, love?" Joanna called down the stairs.

"Yes, it's me. I'm sorry I'm late—I gave a young man a lift."

"Nice young man?"

Joanna came round the corner of the banisters, her round, pussycat face alert with curiosity.

"Too muddy to see. An archaeologist. New Zealander."

"Oh," Joanna said dismissingly, "colonial. Not your type."

"Have you been here long? Were you all right?"

"But yes, my dear, of course. Blissful Mrs F. let me in. Lucky girl, to have all this domestic staff."

"You make her sound like a retinue," Annette said, laughing. "Heavens, however did I manage to get my hair so wet just crossing the sidewalk? Excuse me for two minutes—mix yourself a drink while I give it a rub. There's a fine fire."

"Don't hurry, my dear. We've all the weekend for gossip, after all. And we don't want you catching a cold after your other ailments. You're supposed to be *cosseting* yourself, silly girl—not traipsing around in the wet!"

Annette changed out of her damp trousers and sweater, ran hot water, vigorously towelled her short dark hair. How could she have managed to get so wet in such a short time? What could she have been doing?

She concentrated with all her strength, standing in the bathroom, her eyes fixed unseeingly on the steam-frosted mirror. *Why* couldn't she remember? It was so stupid! It was like sleepwalking—but much more worrying. One minute your mind was with you, yours to command, and then, unaccountably, you found that it had been absent, had travelled away from you and come back from God knows where. Struggling for memory, you found nothing but a blank, nothing but mist.

For Kilmeny had been, she knew not where
And Kilmeny had seen what she could not
declare . . .

She leaned forward, staring at the glass. Behind the globules of steam her pale image moved forward dimly to meet her. With a sudden impatient gesture she rubbed the glass clear, turned sharply on her heel, and ran downstairs.

"Come and chat while I hot up the soup," she called to Joanna, going into the kitchen.

"Doesn't Mrs F. do that? Do you still know how?" jibed Joanna, strolling after, glass in hand, and perching her round, compact but graceful body on the corner of the kitchen table. All that Joanna did was pleasing to the eye: although not one of her features would have won marks in a beauty contest, she was so neat, elegant, and well-groomed that to look at her was as satisfying as looking at a good picture or a well-designed piece of furniture.

"It's Mrs Fairhall's evening off. Busman's holiday. She's helping out at the Bell. Her sister's the cook there, you know, and she likes to go and get the gossip. I expect she's washing up for my young man now."

"He's staying at the Bell, is he?" said Joanna with a twinkle. "He must have some cash then. Doesn't compensate for dullness, though, and he's sure to be dull. Antipodes *and* archaeology—my God, what a combination!—My dear, you do look peaky! You haven't had a relapse, have you? Everyone at the office sent love and said *don't* try to hurry back to work too soon, there's *no* occasion for it. I know one hates to feel one's not indispensable, but really everything's going along on *oiled wheels*, you may take my word for it."

"I'm sure I may," Annette said with a wry grin. "Let's eat by the fire, shall we?" She poured the steaming soup into two bowls and added a dollop of brandy to each.

"And you couldn't do that on a mere, smear salary," said Joanna, sliding off the corner of the table. "Shall I bring this?" She picked up the breadboard and followed Annette.

"My dear, you are making this house *ravishing*. Auntie Loo would turn in her grave if she could see it without the dadoes and antimacassars."

"Wouldn't she approve?"

"Heavens, no! Mutton-chop wallpapers and whiskery upholstery were her line. What you might call period stuff."

"But you like what I've done?" said Annette a little defensively.

"Darling! Of course I do. I think you've worked wonders! I *knew* that buying a little place of your own like this and tinkering about with it would be just the thing to put you back on your feet after that tiresome complaint."

"And that tiresome young man," Annette said, willing her mouth to smile. "Being jilted is so debilitating."

"And that ghastly creature, of course. He, I may say, has been going round the office looking like a hangdog edition of Uriah *Heep*. I think he thought he'd jolted you into a decline. We told him it was nothing of the kind. They breed sterner stuff on *Eyewitness*, I told him. Someone who can keep that lot sane and co-ordinated is not so easy to dismay. All she has, I said, is a case of delayed shock over her windfall. I hope by now that you're coming round to the point of view that it's far better to have all that lovely lolly than to marry a spineless creature who can't stand up to the idea of being thought a fortune hunter?"

"Oh, decidedly," said Annette. Her tone was absent; she was wishing painfully that Joanna had not found it necessary to discuss her with Philip.

In any case—a bitter question that had been troubling her intermittently for the past two months here reared its head again—was it really the fortune that had put Philip off? Had Philip in fact known about the money when he ducked apologetically out of their engagement? Or had he simply been scared of the extra demands that Annette might make on him after the shock of her father's harrowing death?

There had been that odd telephone conversation—during which, for no reason that she could pin down, Annette became convinced that Philip was not alone at his end of the line, that there was somebody else in the background. Philip was laid up with a bad case of grippe and had refused to let her come to his flat in case she caught it.

"You see, dearest," he had said, his voice cracking with sincerity, "I do so want you to be *free*. I'm thinking of *you*, you know that. Just at this time I wouldn't want you to be tied in any way. I wouldn't want to feel that I was preventing you from, for instance, making a complete break, doing something different with your life—"

But don't you see, Annette had wanted to cry out, making a complete break is the *last* thing I want to do just now. I don't want freedom. I want the comfort of ties.

She didn't say it, though. Afraid of alarming Philip by intensifying the emotional atmosphere, she said instead, keeping her voice carefully level, "Well, it's kind of you to think of it that way, Philip; I do see what you mean. We'll call it a pause for reconsideration, shall we?"

"I'm only thinking of you, dearest," he repeated. "This is such a crucial time for you."

Could Philip really be so flat-footed? "Because of the money, you mean?" Annette said.

"Because of the—?"

"My five hundred thousand. My winnings."

"Oh yes. Yes, that of course." But hadn't he sounded taken aback, as if this were the first he'd heard of it? And she remembered that he had been away from the office with his grippe when she'd broken the news to the others. "Excuse me a minute, I can hear my kettle boiling," he added hurriedly and there had been a gap. Could Annette hear low voices in the background? Hard to decide. But by the time Philip came back to the phone she had herself in hand and was able to say calmly:

"Well, maybe you're right, my dear. Perhaps it is for the best that I should have a spell of independence."

"You're so *wise*, dearest."

"Anyway we'll see each other soon at the office, shan't we? Take care of the grippe. . . ." And she had rung off, thankful that she had managed to keep her voice organised, and that telephones were not yet fitted with vision screens. . . .

"Think no more of Philip." Joanna dismissed the subject, piling soup plates on a tray. "What have you done with Auntie Loo's sewing-room?"

"Which was that?"

"The big first-floor room looking out on the garden."

"Oh, that—I'll show you after supper. I'm turning it into a studio."

"Starting to paint again? Industrious girl. I'd better introduce you to my famous old cousin. He lives down here, when he's in England."

"Your famous cousin? Which one's that?" Annette said, handing her visitor a dish of peaches.

"Oh, didn't I ever mention him?" Joanna answered smoothly. "(My *dear!* These look sumptuous!) How very unlike me. I generally blow my family trumpet like anything. He's a painter—not all that old, actually, but so venerated and monumental that when you see him you expect him to be all covered over with graffiti, like Stonehenge."

"Not Crispin James?"

"Why, yes. Did you know he had a house down here?" said Joanna with a faint air of gratification. "The old boy *will* be pleased."

"Well, of course. The way one knows Churchill lives at Chartwell."

"Darling, you look quite awestruck. What fun this is. You two must certainly meet. He'll be delighted to know he has a young colleague living in the town. Most of the natives, I need hardly say, he regards as less than beneath *contempt*. They are pretty abysmal. As you probably know, Cris spends ninety per cent of his time abroad. What a piece of luck that he's not long come over from Paris for one of his duty tours. I'm sure he'll find you a kindred spirit."

This seemed so unlikely that Annette couldn't help suspecting her dear friend of some disingenuousness. But no doubt it was kindly meant.

How extraordinary, though, of Joanna never to have mentioned that she had this famous connection! How very restrained! Most people would hardly be able to resist boasting of such a feather in the family cap, even if the boast took the form of an elegant disclaimer—"Of course he's much too grand to recognise *our* branch." But for Joanna—subtle, sober Joanna—even such a form of allusion, apparently, would transgress the boundaries of good taste. Perhaps in the office, among the *Sweet Home* staff, she had felt it a necessity to keep the relationship dark in case she was pressed to secure special interviews and preferential treatment. That would be the reason, no doubt. But all the same, what strength of character it betokened. Annette looked at her friend with new and greater respect.

"He lives down on the Mediterranean coast a lot of the time, doesn't he?" she said.

"Oh, all *around*, my dear. He was in Germany for ages. And in Mexico. To tell you the *truth*, among other things in England he couldn't stick my Auntie Loo. Kin, maybe, but decidedly less than kind. So when she died I daresay he came back hotfoot. I suppose she was about the *one* person who didn't regard him with the proper *reverence*. Sure as fate, if ever he did come back to Crowbridge, she was certain to rile him in some way—of course in a little town like this you're always meeting people even if you haven't the least intention of doing so; he hadn't entered her house for about twenty years, but there was some horrific occasion when they met in the post office and she told him that his work was deteriorating *rapidly*. My dear, the bystanders said it was the most frightening thing they had *ever seen*—he picked up an inkstand and dashed it on the floor and the P.M. hadn't the courage to make him pay for the *mess*. Auntie Loo, of course, just stalked out, not the least impressed; quite a pair of *characters*."

"I believe you," Annette said, smiling. Now she thought

about it, she believed, too, that she could detect a resemblance between Crispin James and his younger cousin Joanna, who herself had no small reputation for character, brainpower, and formidable ability in the office. She was of parallel rank with Annette, editing a magazine that dealt with furnishing and interior decoration; Annette had heard that her staff went in terror of her mordant tongue.

"My dear, I'm madly sleepy," Joanna said, elegantly stifling a yawn. "I think I must totter off to my tiny bed. May I help myself to a hot-water bottle? Old country habits die hard, though I can feel you keep the house a *thousand* times warmer than it was in days of yore. . . . I do think this claret-and-white-grapey wallpaper round the stairwell is perfectly be*witching*. Oh, I *am* so glad I told you Auntie Loo's house was for sale. You will just have to keep fending me off, I can tell you, or I shall be foisting myself on you every single weekend."

"You'd be welcome, of course," Annette said, feeling her neck in a preoccupied way. "I'm so glad you like what I'm doing."

"Stiff neck, darling?"

"It feels a bit stiff, yes—I can't think why."

"Better wrap up snug and take a vitamin C tablet," advised Joanna. "We don't want you relapsing and having any more of those dizzy spells. You've been going on better, though, haven't you? Beginning to get used to your affluence? No more blackouts?"

". . . No."

"And the doctor down here is a decent old croaker, isn't he?"

"Dr Whitney? Yes, he seems very nice."

"Ah well, he'll keep an eye on you. Good night, my love." Joanna disappeared into her bedroom.

"Good night."

Annette had decorated her room in black and white. White walls, white woolly carpet, black beams, zebra-striped curtains. She crossed to the mirror, ran her fingers through her dark hair, staring at her reflection, which stared frowningly back: a pointed face, pale now, with wide, generous mouth and black smudges beneath the eyes. Once again her hand moved uncertainly to her throat.

How had they come there? Those dark bruises on the paler skin beneath the line of her jaw?

II

The gale freshened during the night. Rain dashed against Annette's diamond-paned windows and the wind whistled and keened among the pointed roofs and television aerials of the little marshland town. Annette lay wakeful, wondering if the storm would find weak places in her five-hundred-year-old roof, and then grinned at her automatic habit of worrying. Heaven knows there's enough money to patch up a hole or two, she thought drowsily; I must get out of this trick of waking up in the small hours to brood.

With the skill of several months' practice she steered her mind past the memory of Philip—handsome, specious Philip, so affectionate, so sympathetic, so all-fired plausible.

After the telephone conversation she had not seen him for two or three weeks. The prolonged strain of her father's painful illness and death had suddenly taken effect and she had fainted dead away at a press lunch. When she came to it was to find herself in a nursing home, in an oxygen tent, with pneumonia complicated by jaundice.

For a fortnight she had refused to receive any visitors. Her pride, which she had stiffened against pity or covert curiosity in the office, could not endure this final blow, this public shame of collapse into a visible green-and-yellow melancholy. With stony indifference she eyed the cards from colleagues, the flowers, the messages, the baskets of fruit. But in the end Joanna had wheedled her way in, solicitous, friendly, not too commiserating, the ideal companion for a convalescent, cheering Annette with an easily digested froth of lighthearted gossip. It was Joanna who had organised Annette's final emergence from hospital—not back to the flat, with its bleak memories, but to a comfortable hotel.

Joanna, with her twinkling common sense, had managed to make the whole process of recovery seem, not painless, but at least unimportant, by cushioning every detail with cheerful nonsense. It was Joanna, too, who came up with the suggestion that, as Annette still required a couple of months' convalescence, she should pass the interval pleasantly and not too idly in Crowbridge, purchasing the cottage of Joanna's Auntie Loo, recently deceased. What fun it would be, she said, to redecorate it up to *Sweet Home* standards! And then it could always be sold again, at a handsome profit, of course. She had borrowed a car and driven the reluctant Annette down to Crowbridge to look at the place.

Crowbridge, in its salty wind-swept isolation, beyond miles of sea-marsh, had caught at Annette's imagination. It was beautiful and anachronistic, a slice out of *then*, an enclave from some earlier century. Annette was touched, unexpectedly shaken out of apathy. And the little house in Crossbow Lane had clinched the matter.

"There, you see!" Joanna said self-congratulatingly. "I *knew* you'd love it." Her plump clever face sparkled with satisfaction. "I tell you what, we won't let the agent guess that you're the Annette Sheldon who won all the money; otherwise, my dear, he'd *treble* the price. I'll just introduce you as my hard-working office buddy who wants to buy the place as cheaply as possible. I'll *denigrate* it. After all I know every cracked pane and patch of dry-rot *intimately*. I used to stay with Auntie Loo—she was a cousin really, but Auntie seemed a more appropriate epithet—whenever my parents were getting divorced."

"But won't you be doing yourself down? Doesn't the cottage come to you?"

"My dear, no! You didn't know my Auntie Loo or you wouldn't have supposed a thing like that. She was such a fun-loving old lady—always one for a joke, and some of them were not altogether *good-natured*. No, my dear, you're not depriving me of a thing; it merely comes out of the estate, about which, candidly, I couldn't care *less.*"

So the house had been bought, if not quite for a song, at least, as Joanna said, not for one of the Top Ten. The negotiations had gone through with dreamlike smoothness and ease, and in what seemed no time at all Annette had found herself installed. She had refused to stay at the Bell and had moved right in, camping in one room or another as workmen surged about the house replacing patches of dry-rot. Meanwhile she scoured salerooms and antique stores all over the country for the kind of period furniture she wanted.

During all this time she had seen Philip only once, when, visiting London for a few days on business, she had called at the office to collect some personal belongings. Her mind still winced a little at the recollection of that final meeting.

Out of shame for herself? she wondered. Or for Philip?

"If only we'd got married three months ago," he had said ruefully. "If only we were on our honeymoon now, darling, it would be different. But to marry you after you've got that damned great windfall—I can't, I simply can't face the thought of what people will say about my motives."

At least he knew his own weaknesses. One had to hand that to him.

"I could give the money to charity." Annette's tone was dry.

"Oh, no, that would be crazy," he said quickly. "No, it's just my tragedy and I must learn to live with it. You'll find someone a thousand times better than me, Annette dear."

Your tragedy, my friend? What about mine? And at lunch the very next day she had seen him over in the far corner of the Rosenkavalier with a very pretty red-headed girl, gay as a lark, obviously from relief. So what was one to make of that? Annette thought wryly. It's galling enough to be thrown over, but still more so to be given the air with five hundred thousand in one's pocket.

In an attempt to banish Philip's charming, smiling, protesting image—heavens, yes, that was the worst of it; even now, though she knew him inside out, the thought of him gave her a terrible wrench: he was such fun to be with; his charm was irresistible when he turned on the full battery—Annette let her mind slip back with discomfort to something that had been half consciously fretting her ever since she woke: the memory of that dangling rope in the car, one end tied to the spare tyre. A reef knot. I always make a reef. And pools of water in the trunk, as if I'd been carrying something big, with the lid open. But what? Something I'd bought at the auction? And if so, where is it? Could it have worked loose and fallen off? I'd gone over to Broadsea to look at greenhouse heaters, called at the furniture sale in Long Green, and came back through Meresham Woods—I remember the colours of the trees. But what happened then? Did I stop somewhere else? At the antique shop in Meresham? Or at old Mrs Munday's? I meant to look for a rocking chair—did I find one? Was that what I had tied in the back? And if so where is it now?

She frowned, lying stiffly in bed, staring at the blackness of the ceiling and listening to the buffeting of the wind. She tried to visualise a chair, a rocking chair, tethered to the car by a bit of rope, but the picture would not come right; the spindle-back formed itself into an ugly square and the rockers obstinately curved round into wheels—what nonsense, as if she'd buy a wheel-chair! No use, no use at all, Annette thought despairingly. It's horrible—terrifying—like going blind. Can one go blind in one's mind?

There's a technical word for that, a small chill voice suggested, the word used by psychiatrists. . . .

Crash! The relentless wind had at last found a yielding prey and worried loose something big, something heavy, which had fallen into Annette's garden with a cascading tinkle of broken glass. Glad of the distraction she jumped out of bed, found a flashlight, and leaned out of the window, sending the torch-beam down through driving rain and thrashing branches. The pool of light travelled across the lawn and presently found what she expected: a window blown down, casement and all, but not one of hers, all of which had diamond panes. This must be one from next door. It was lying twisted and shattered on the wet, glistening grass.

Annette's room had windows on two sides, and the second window, which carried an admonitory placard "Ancient Lights" beneath it, looked out on the neglected next-door garden and had a diagonal view of the back of the next-door house. Flicking her torch-beam up and down its façade, Annette was puzzled. All the windows seemed to be in place. But the thin knitting-needle of light felt its way upwards, climbing the stone wall to the angle of the roof, right up to the attic window in the gable, and there, instead of the reflecting flash of glass, found nothing but a square black hole.

I wonder if they know their window's gone? Annette thought. How odd to keep it open at night in a storm.

Yes, somebody obviously did know and was inspecting the damage, for a flicker of white showed behind what looked like bars in the opening. A child's room, perhaps? Not that Annette had ever seen any children issuing from the house next door—for the matter of that, she had never seen her neighbours at all. Anyway, whoever it was presumably had the situation in hand and would not have to be roused and told about it.

Yawning, she switched off her torch and went back to bed, this time to sleep.

"What a night!" said plump, cheerful Mrs Fairhall, putting a tray with coffee, grapes, melon, pineapple, tangerines, beside Joanna's bed, and going across to swish back the curtains. "Did you wake much, Miss Joanna?"

"No, I slept like the dead." Joanna stretched luxuriously in bed. "What a blissful tray, Mrs F. You've certainly remembered my tastes."

"Miss Annette did that." The woman cast a disapproving glance at the mass of fruit. "Have you remembered plenty of greengroceries, Mrs F.? says she. Oh, says I, it's Miss Joanna this weekend with her fancy ways, is it, I says, plain honest-to-goodness meat and puddings was good enough for her auntie, old Miss James, I says, none of this finigling fruit diet. *You* ain't so picking in your ways, Miss Annette, says I, and thankful I am to see you putting a bit of flesh on your bones."

"How do you think she is—Miss Sheldon?" Joanna said, rather nettled at this rapid promotion to "Miss Annette" of someone who was, after all, an outsider, not part of the family.

"Not too bad. She has her peaky days and her worrying spells, of course. You worry too much, Miss Annette, about things that can't be helped, says I. You want to get out more, join the golf club, meet people. All in good time, says she. And I must say, she's not one to mope, always busy with something in the house or going off hunting for furniture—only sometimes I'll catch her with that look on her face—"

"What look?" Joanna asked curiously.

But the flood of Mrs Fairhall's loquacity had suddenly dried up, she gave Joanna a suspicious glance and said, "Will you be wanting some more coffee, Miss Joanna, or is what's there enough?"

A sudden joyful burst of orchestral music from downstairs almost drowned Joanna's reply.

"It's the man testing the new radiogram," Mrs Fairhall explained in response to Joanna's lifted eyebrows. "The time it's taken her to make up her mind to get that, and she loves a bit of music! Go on, it's your money, I've said to her time and again, you're only here once, but Mrs F, says she, I can't get used to spending and that's a fact."

"I bet it won't take her long, just the same," Joanna said dryly.

Mrs Fairhall's eyes flashed, "I'll tell you one thing she has done, Miss Joanna. She's given money to the council to build half a dozen old people's bungalows. And that's something your Auntie Loo would never have done."

"No, she wouldn't," Joanna agreed good-temperedly.

"The old so-and-so never thought of anybody but herself."

But when Mrs Fairhall had left the room Joanna got up in a mood of considerable irritation and began pacing to and fro, lighting one cigarette from the stub of the last. "Old people's bungalows!" she muttered angrily. "What stupidity will she spend it on next?" And presently she went down to the little telephone room under the stairs and made a call.

"Where's Miss Sheldon?" she asked, emerging to find Mrs Fairhall busy with a duster.

"Gone to the doctor's surgery." The woman pursed her lips disapprovingly. "If I've told her once I've told her a dozen times, Miss Annette, dear, ask him to come here and he'll come, same as he always did for Miss James. But, no, she says, I'm used to not giving people extra trouble and I'll go on that way."

"Very proper too," said Joanna cheerfully. "But what's the trouble? Isn't she feeling well?"

"Oh, just her regular check-up." Mrs Fairhall's tone was vague.

"Well, I'm going to do some shopping. Perhaps I'll meet her in the town. If not I shan't be long, tell her."

The storm was gone, the sun was hot, and the cobbles in the street shone sleek as jewels. Virginia creeper was a tattered scarlet against old stone walls. The tourist watercolour painters were out in full force with their campstools and their easels. Joanna chuckled inwardly as she passed a couple of earnest dabblers in bulky tweeds and soup-plate hats, parked worshipfully at the entrance to Bell Street.

"So wonderfully medieval, isn't it," one lady said to the other, peering with vague dissatisfaction at her watery sketch-block. She rinsed her brush in a meat-paste jar, shaking drops of slaty liquid about the street, and tried again. "One finds it hard to reproduce that exact vermilion tint."

Joanna imagined Crispin James's castigating comments.

The surgery waiting-room was a period piece. Oak floor and panelling, polished with age to a lustrous black, reflected the russets and greens of the garden beyond the mullioned window, where shrubs bordered the walls and a walnut tree in the middle of a mossy lawn stood in a pool of its own fallen leaves. A Tudor queen might have sat there without incongruity.

One ought to be able to be healthy in a place like this, Annette thought. People probably live into their nineties, if not their hundreds. Idly wandering about the room, she read a framed and engraved certificate which hung between the windows. It announced to the world that Frdrck Theophilus Frazer, M.D., of St. Andrews University, Phyfician, was qualified to Practife Chirurgerie, Furgerie, Cupping, Leeching, and the Minor Medical Artf.

Good for old Frdrck Theophilus. She wondered how long he had gone on prescribing his pills and boluses to the citizens of Crowbridge. For all she knew he was at it still, practising his minor medical artf, senior partner to Dr Whitney (himself no chicken).

But the surgery itself, when she reached the head of the queue and walked through, was reassuringly modern in equipment and appearance, though the same hushed and fragrant garden could be seen from its windows.

"Well, my dear young lady! And what can I do for you? I'm delighted to observe that our good air is beginning to put a bit of colour into your cheeks. Little by little, here an inch and there an inch, eh? that's the way. You're looking a trifle tired, though, which I don't like to see. What seems to be the trouble?"

Dr Whitney was big and silver-haired and fatherly—a little too fatherly, Annette sometimes felt. She struggled against the inclination to find something faintly bogus about him. But he was a good doctor, no doubt of that.

"Are you taking the tonic I gave you?" he inquired solicitously.

"Yes, I'm taking it." Annette's tone was weary. She lay back in the armchair. Dr Whitney eyed her with professional care. His rather small grey eyes were half covered, most of the time, by their pouched lower lids, giving him a faintly reptilian appearance. But when his eyes opened wide their expression was extremely shrewd.

"You're worrying too much," he admonished Annette. "Fussing and fretting about that job of yours and trying to measure your recovery by hours and minutes instead of just placidly vegetating. You need to take things easy, my dear young lady. Get out more, get the benefit of this marvellous sea air, meet people, stop brooding. Forget about the office."

"That's what I'm afraid of."

"How do you mean, my dear?"

"Forgetting." She stared at him miserably. "Dr Whitney, it *terrifies* me. How can I feel I'm getting well if every now and then I suddenly find that I can't remember a thing about what I've just been doing—that an hour, two hours of the day are just a total blank? How can I even think of going back to the office? And I do want to, you know. I'm not made for an idle life; my career is important to me. I—I want to feel there's some justification for my existence."

Dr Whitney was gallant. "My dear, what other justification would be needed for such a pretty and charming member of your sex?" He raised a hand, unperturbed, as she started to protest. "Patience, patience. You mustn't think of going back yet. Not till you've put on a bit more weight. You're still slightly anaemic too, you know." He leaned forward and flipped down her eyelid. "You mustn't forget that you were quite seriously ill. The excitement of winning the money—hmn, yes—and your father's sad death—you've had a great deal to withstand, my dear. Some setbacks must be expected. But you're a very lucky girl—job being kept for you, no financial worries. As for that other trouble, it's nothing, nothing at all. Happens in dozens of cases. Just as soon as you begin to relax and enjoy yourself it will stop. I'll give you a prescription for some sleeping-tablets to help. You'll soon see a difference."

"But I can't relax. I keep wondering if I shall forget

something really important or do something queer when I'm having one of these blackouts."

"You won't do anything queer. You're a decent, law-abiding citizen. People go on behaving in character, whatever the circumstances. And you won't forget anything important. That's the beauty of this blessed place, my dear," said Dr Whitney. "Nothing ever happens in it, so there's nothing to forget." He smiled at her with infinite reassurance.

Noel Hanaker sat in his oak-floored, oak-beamed, gabled hotel bedroom, pen in hand, and stared at the view from the window. It was a superb view. Immediately below him the roofs of Crowbridge dropped steeply downhill and beyond their twisted Tudor chimneys and the encircling town wall the marsh stretched—wide, flat, sunswept and hazy, criss-crossed with dykes—to a thin shining line which looked like the world's edge but was in fact the sea.

It was all very beautiful—oak beams, Tudor chimneys, ancient trees, immemorial marshes. Sometimes you can have too much beauty, Noel thought sourly. It's like a diet of jam—you begin to pine for something tough and plain to get your teeth into.

Deliberately he moved his chair, turning his back on the view.

"Dear Jill," he wrote, "It's being harder than I expected. England is so small and so packed and so old and so mixed-up. Scratch the ground and you may find a Queen Anne sixpence or a flint arrowhead. Scratch a human being and you find the lord knows what—they are as complicated and full of secrets as a Chinese puzzle. Still, I'm making progress. I'm down here at Crowbridge now and at last I've met the legendary Crispin James. He seems the most complicated of all. . . ."

His pen stopped moving and he gazed broodingly at a tarnished silver coin that lay in a collection of archaeological finds on a sheet of blotting-paper.

He got up, crossed the room, and took from his wallet

on the bedside table two small pieces of paper that appeared to have been roughly torn from a pocket diary. The date on them was over a year old:

> Too tired to get up today. Sent the boy out for a bottle of cognac and I'm lying in bed drinking it and listening to the rain on the skylight. Why doesn't that devil come back? Just for a weekend, he said, and now it's a month, two months—I can't remember. I'm in a muddle. And then the letter, 'Wait, remember your promise.' What promise? I don't remember making one. But I'm waiting—only I don't know what for.
>
> Cognac is good. It helps. It keeps me warm and I'm really waiting very patiently. The rain is coming through the hole in the ceiling now and dripping into a bucket—tap, tap, tap. Strangely enough it seems to remind me of something, but I can't decide what.
>
> I think perhaps I am dying. I have a queer feeling that at twelve o'clock . . .

Here the writing stopped.

At twelve o'clock. What had happened at twelve o'clock?

Noel read and reread the scraps of handwriting as he had twenty times before, and then sighed and put the torn pages carefully back in his wallet. He tucked it in his windbreaker pocket, buttoned the flap, and prepared to go downstairs to the bar. Before doing so he slipped his unfinished letter into a copy of Somervell's *Domestic Roman Architecture in East Anglia and the Home Counties.*

As he closed his bedroom door the church clock was striking twelve.

Returning home after her visit to the doctor, Annette noticed that the neighbour's attic window was still lying smashed in the middle of her lawn. She called to Fairhall, who was pruning, and asked if anyone had been round about it.

"That'll be Mrs Kundry's window," he said, squinting up at the next-door house. "Attic, that be. Reckon she hasn't noticed it yet. Doesn't stir out much in the mornings, Mrs Kundry doesn't."

Annette asked him to remove the wreckage, and then pushed open the next-door gate. It had a loud unpleasing squeak.

"They can't use it a lot," she thought. "One could hear that all up the street, but I don't remember noticing it. Perhaps there's a back gate. Though I don't quite see how there can be. Her garden ends at the town wall, just like mine."

The brick-paved front path was mossy and weed-grown; the small railed-in front garden had not been tended for years and was a tangle of sodden grass and dead leaves from the overgrown lilacs. A gleam of pink caught Annette's eye, something lying by the path in a tussock of grass. It was a baby's plastic rattle. She picked it up. The people next door had children then? But there were no diapers on the clothes-line, never any sound of a child's presence. Perhaps the rattle had been dropped by a caller's baby?

She rang the doorbell.

After a fairly long wait—Annette had begun to wonder if the inmates were out—the door was opened by a thin, elderly woman who gave a convulsive start, apparently at the sight of Annette standing on her doorstep with the pink rattle in her hands.

This, thought Annette, couldn't be the baby's mother. She must be at least fifty-five, probably more—a frail, wispy, grey-haired woman who seemed to be in the last extremities of fright at the appearance of her visitor. Why? To the best of her knowledge Annette had never seen her before. Perhaps she was afraid that her window had done damage and she might have to pay for it?

"Good morning," Annette said pleasantly. "Are you Mrs Kundry? I'm your new neighbour, Annette Sheldon, as you probably know. I called round to ask if you knew that your attic window had blown out in the night. Wasn't it a terrible gale? I expected to find that half of my tiles were off, but I suppose down here you're used to winds like that."

Why was the woman looking at her with that fixed, fascinated stare?

"Oh by the way, is this yours?" Annette dangled the pink rattle on her finger. "I found it by the path." She tried to smile, but the little woman's rigidity of expression defeated her.

"Oh yes." The words came out in a whisper. So she was at least able to speak. "Yes, it's not mine, but I know whose it is." She put out a violently shaking hand for the rattle and its plastic bells quivered as she took it from Annette. "Thank you very much."

"And you did know about the window? It was on my lawn, but completely smashed, I'm afraid—Fairhall says it isn't worth saving."

"Oh, thank you. Yes I did know. My daughter—" she bit off the words and started again. "I'm sorry it fell on your lawn."

"Oh heavens, that's all right. You couldn't help it. Don't give it a thought. Have you someone who can put in another?"

"Yes thank you. Was—"

Annette felt she was going to say, "Was that all you came for?" but instead, with a gasp, she brought out, "Wasn't it an awful storm?" and laid her hand nervously on the door handle, glancing over her shoulder.

"Awful. Well—if you're sure I can't do anything—"

"No. Oh no, thanks all the same."

Annette gave her a cheerful smile and walked quickly down the garden path. Poor thing, it seemed too hard to keep her palpitating in her doorway any longer.

"Perhaps she had a lover hidden behind the pram in the front porch," quipped Joanna when Annette told her about this odd interview.

"There *was* no pram."

"Well then, that's it. Her daughter, who is grown up, has had an illegitimate child and they're desperate to keep it a secret."

"They do that all right," said Annette. "It was the first time I'd seen *her*, let alone the daughter. They never seem to go anywhere in the town."

"Perhaps she's seen you before when you didn't see her—obviously at the Infant Welfare or somewhere compromising," suggested Joanna cheerfully. "Or while she was visiting her daughter in prison."

"What was I doing in prison?"

"Taking good books to the inmates."

Was it fancy, or did Annette detect under Joanna's light tone a skilled, relentless probing—like the geologist's tap with his hammer, seeking the flaw in the rock? *Had* she ever seen Mrs Kundry before? she asked herself. And if so, where?

Joanna's light-coloured eyes were on her, after the first flicker steady and bright as topazes.

"More likely she'd been picking flowers in my garden and had a bad conscience," Annette said. "There's quite a well-worn path that connects the two gardens at the back, along under the rampart wall. I suppose she was a friend of your Auntie Loo. —I don't know about you, but I'm ravenous. I thought we'd go and have lunch at the Bell. . . .

At lunch Joanna began working through a report on progress at the office. Normally Joanna had nothing to do with *Eyewitness*, the newsmagazine that Annette edited, but she had been put in charge of it as well as her own department until Annette was pronounced better.

She dealt out bits of information with reluctance, as if all was so smoothly in train that it was hardly worth describing, but every now and then something she said stuck a little pinprick of disquiet into Annette's mind.

"What about the cover? Christmas has gone to press, I suppose; what about the following issue?"

"We got Volage to do some reindeer."

"But didn't you find my file—the ski-jump?"

"No," said Joanna, looking blank. "There was nothing marked up for that issue. Harris didn't know of any."

"But I had covers scheduled for the whole year—"

"Maybe they went astray," said Joanna, shrugging. "Naturally I'll have another look—but there have been so many inquests . . ." She let the awkward pause lengthen and then added briskly, "Of course, poor love, there was such *mayhem* the first couple of weeks after you fell ill, before they pushed me over there, with your not very bright staff trying to cope—I expect they thought the covers were artists' samples, or something, and sent them back."

"Kate and Harris are very intelligent people," Annette said, trying to sound indulgent to Joanna's exaggeration.

"Well, maybe I scare them."

Annette looked at her watch. She wasn't really interested in finding out the hour; it was merely an unconscious manifestation of her wish that time would pass, taking Joanna with it, that the weekend would be over and she could hasten on with the process of trying to get well before her work was taken away from her and her staff terrorised into resigning.

"Well, hullo there! Fine to see you, Miss Sheldon.

Joanna bristled with disapproval of the tall young man in the muddy jacket. All her defences were up at once. But Annette hailed him with something approaching relief as he came up to their table.

"Hullo. I was sure you'd be at your site all day."

"You forget my two punctures. I put in the morning doing some writing up. I'm going out there this afternoon."

"Noel Hanaker, Joanna Southley," Annette said. "Joanna puts the gloss on a glossy monthly called *Sweet Home*."

"Glass furniture and wooden wineglasses," he said, nodding. "Pretty soon they'll be getting right back to the sort of stuff I dig up. I'm pleased to meet you ladies because now I can buy you that drink I owe you, Miss Sheldon. How about a brandy?"

"That would be most sustaining," Joanna said primly,

anticipating Annette. Evidently she had decided that Mr Hanaker was harmless.

They took their brandies and coffee into the garden of the inn, where dahlias blazed in the autumn sunshine.

"I forgot to tell you, Annette," Joanna said, "I called up Crispin this morning and he was *devastatingly* sorry not to be able to meet you this weekend, but he's tied up with some tiresome people over at Tildenby and won't be back till late tomorrow. So I told him to look you up next week."

"Oh, you shouldn't have bothered," Annette said uncomfortably. "I'm sure he'd be bored. I'm such small beer to him."

"*Nonsense*, darling. He loves people who paint."

"Is that Mr Crispin James?" Noel said. When Joanna nodded, smiling, he remarked, "I had the honour of dining with him last night."

"Oh, so you did, of course," Annette said. "Did you get on well?" She overlooked Joanna's suddenly startled, wary expression, but Mr Hanaker caught it and said easily, "He seemed a very pleasant guy. Do you know him well, Miss Southley?"

"We're cousins," Joanna said. "Had you met him before?"

"No, but he knew my brother in Paris."

"*How* interesting," Joanna said. She gave Noel a brilliant insincere smile, glanced at her watch and cried, "Annette, love, I'm going to *drag* you away for your rest, because this afternoon I want to go over to Wildernesse and buy you an expensive, foolish present for the house, so we must be off."

"I'd hoped you might come and look at my site," Noel said.

"Another time we'd adore to." She flashed the smile again and whisked Annette away. "*What* a dull young man," she said when they were out in Bell Street. "It's to be hoped he won't stay here long."

"I thought he was rather nice."

"He's a dead bore and we must pray that you aren't afflicted with too much of him. You only think him pleasant because you've been rusticating and have forgotten what lively company is like."

And for the rest of the day Joanna was such lively company herself that Annette almost forgot how uncomfortable her dear friend sometimes made her feel.

"You needn't bother looking up trains for me," Joanna said airily on Sunday afternoon, as they were returning from a stroll round the empty, sunny streets. "Philip very kindly volunteered to drive me back, as he's weekending with friends not too far away. He's coming over for me at five."

"Philip?"

"Now don't go all tense on me, darling. You know you and Philip had to meet again sometime, and I thought this would be the kindest way, out of range of prying office eyes."

Annette supposed the arrangement had been made with good intentions, but her ex-fiancé was the last person she wanted to see. Curiously enough, what troubled her most was her looks; she had convinced herself that Philip was of no importance, but still it was depressing that he should see her looking thin and pale and lacking the benefit of a decent hairdresser.

"I wish you'd told me yesterday," she said. "I'd have gone to Broadsea and had my hair done. Better for morale."

"Nonsense, darling, you look like a million dollars. A bit more lipstick and you'd win a beauty contest."

Annette grinned at this palpable overstatement. However, it did her morale good—a little—to see Philip's convertible limping uncomfortably over the cobbles of Crossbow Lane like a large athlete making his painful barefoot way over a shingle-bank, and she was able to greet Philip himself with composure when he came in, looking a trifle sheepish.

Philip was tall and slight; his awkward coltish grace seemed touchingly immature until one remembered with surprise that he was thirty, not nineteen; hazel-brown hair flopped engagingly over his forehead and he had a long, weak, obstinate, charming chin, a violinist's chin; while they were engaged Annette used to twit him that he ought to have taken up the trombone and blown some strength into his chin instead of pushing it back all the time with his fiddle; he accepted her teasing with total good-nature, but since the break Annette had more than once taken herself to task for lack of sensitivity. His eyes were his best feature: large, grey, and full of intelligence. Stifling a pang at their responsive liveliness, Annette thought, Why must intelligent, faithless people always be so much better company than the kind, dull, reliable sort? I daresay Crowbridge is full of good citizens with impeccable characters, and I'd swap days of their conversation for a couple of hours' argument over layouts with the *Eyewitness* planning team.

"Hullo, Philip," she said lightly. "Martini?"

"Hullo, my dear. Marvellous to see you looking so much better. I say, you have done wonders here, haven't you? Full marks, my dear. I'd hardly have known it for the same place."

"Why, had you been here before?" said Annette, surprised.

"Oh, ages ago. There was some notion, once, about getting pictures of Miss James's garden for a feature on creepers. But it came to nought. The old lady rather took against me, didn't she, Joanna? You'd thought she'd be amused by the creeper idea and being in the pages of *Sweet Home*, but she denounced it as vulgar publicity."

"Philip, I think we really ought to be on our way; time's hastening along," Joanna said smoothly, glancing at her watch.

"Oh, of course, we've a dinner date with those people, haven't we? But don't worry, my dear, I'll drive like the wind. We'll easily make it. Where's your case? I'll take it out to the car."

He smiled placatingly at Joanna who seemed, for some reason, slightly put out.

Annette reflected that Joanna and Philip seemed, all of a sudden, to be becoming very thick together. Previously, in the office, they had never, to the best of her recollection, had much to say to one another. The story of Auntie Loo's creepers was news to her. But it was, after all, none of her affair.

"Goodbye, my love," said Joanna, embracing her warmly. "Thank you for a blissful weekend, and I'll write. Don't worry about the silly office; all the things I've mentioned have been mere *trifles.* And amuse yourself well with my horrid cousin Crispin—he's really great fun. But he wants a woman's settling influence sadly."

She blew Annette kisses through the windscreen, the car lumbered off over the cobbles, and then they were gone.

III

Annette walked indoors, left with the fag-end of the week-end, and settled down by the log fire, trying not to think about the office. In spite of herself she was deeply troubled by the various bits of news that had emerged over the last two days. Was Joanna trying by subtle methods to show her, Annette, up as incompetent, inefficient, incapable of doing her job? The person on the spot had such an advantage over the absentee in that respect: things could be twisted, rearranged so as to point to apparent negligence.

Material could be lost—like the covers which had so mysteriously gone astray. Contributors could be antagonised so that they failed to produce their best work. Printers, likewise, could be needled; Annette had always prided herself on the excellent relations she succeeded in maintaining with the printing side, but from one or two stories Joanna had let fall she gathered that these had deteriorated alarmingly, that the printers were now hostile and un-cooperative, producing slipshod work which the editorial staff, according to Joanna, were too inept to catch in time and put right.

But was all this really so? She could hardly suspect Joanna of purposeful sabotage? Or had she misread Joanna's elliptical, inconclusive remarks, with their trick of over-exaggeration? Joanna could not have *meant* to disturb and upset, but her love of a satiric twist to an anecdote had perhaps run away with her, making things seem worse than they were. Annette comforted herself with this supposition. And, after all, Joanna *was* very efficient—she would not deliberately let the magazine go downhill (unless it constituted a threat to her own?) All her own departments ran like clockwork—if her staff was ruled by terror of her biting tongue rather than by affection, at least the results were admirable. But Annette, who believed that equally good results could be obtained by arousing people's enthusiasm, felt her heart bleed for her own hard-working, devoted team. When, for God's sake, *when* would she be fit enough to take up command again?

Never, if you don't relax and take things a bit easier, she told herself, annoyed to discover that she was walking restlessly up and down the pleasant firelit room, oblivious of its charm. She sat down by the fire again and picked up a thriller. It was new, much praised for its impossible-to-put-down grip; she had got it out from the library and saved it against the inevitable reaction of anticlimax and depression after Joanna's departure.

After reading a chapter she realised she had not taken in more than half a dozen sentences. How long would Harris, for instance, remain calm under Joanna's regime? He was brilliant but his temperament was insecure, wildly unstable; if Joanna bothered him into a nerve storm . . . Harris could never do himself justice under attack; he needed coaxing to produce his strokes of genius. And Kate was a gentle creature, easily frightened and made unhappy; Kate had family worries too—oh, damn, damn, damn. Would a letter to Joanna pointing out these facts have any effect? Or would she merely laugh at it? "Annette thinks I don't mollycoddle her staff enough; she believes in a regime of zoo excursions and cream buns every Saturday . . ." No, a letter to Joanna might be fatal. A letter to the director of the group of magazines, then? Would look as if she were going behind Joanna's back, trying to stir up trouble. Oh, damn, damn, damn, damn.

The church-bells rang gloomily for evensong; otherwise there was not a sound in the town. Annette thought of Philip and Joanna, lively and gay, driving back to a dinner party in London. Were they talking about her? What were they saying?

The telephone rang.

Annette was not yet conditioned to her secluded country life in which a telephone call could only be the butcher, or the doctor, or the Mothers' Union asking if she would join; she still felt a prick of expectation as she heard the bell.

The telephone room was a tiny closet under the stairs with a round window like a porthole. One of Annette's own pictures—a fantastic view of a public garden—hung opposite the window. Joanna had been in here making a call, Annette noticed—two of her red-stained filter tips lay in the glass ash-tray.

"Miss Sheldon?" said the harsh, resonant voice. "Crispin James here."

Annette was temporarily deprived of speech, completely at a loss. A series of images passed through her photographic memory: newspaper pictures of the celebrated painter. Crispin James, a severe profile against a broken column in the Roman campagna after his famous audience with the Pope—snapped in spring sunshine, absorbedly reading a tattered paperback with a background of Seine barges—standing to reply to a toast, finger tips on the table, in full regalia of white tie and the cross of the *Légion d'honneur,* serenely ready to make hay of an Academy dinner.

"That *is* Miss Sheldon, isn't it?"

"Oh, yes," she said. "Yes it is. Good evening."

"I was sorry to be tied up while my cousin was staying with you. But if you are free this evening I wondered if you'd care to come and watch the start of a barge race."

"Why yes. I—I'd love to."

"Good. I'll be round for you in ten minutes. Wrap up warmly—there's a sharpish wind." The telephone clicked.

And that's that, thought Annette, staring dazedly at the receiver still in her hand. She felt as if she had dipped a finger into water and been swept away, willy-nilly, by a powerful current. Returning with an effort to the normal, rather cool dry climate of her mind, she reflected that it was a good thing she hadn't answered the phone with dripping new-washed hair and a towel round her head; it seemed likely that she would have accepted his invitation just the same.

She ran upstairs and put on trousers and a thick coat. Before she had finished tying a handkerchief round her head his car was outside, the gong-bell in the front hall faintly boomed, and she heard Mrs Fairhall answer the door.

She ran down the stairs and felt how odd it was to see the tall, silver-haired figure, so familiar from photographs, in her own familiar hall—like a clever piece of montage. But the photographs did not convey the quality of his eyes.

"Good," he said, studying her rig; "you won't get cold in that lot. Joanna said you had been ill." And then, with a faint smile, "We seem to have skipped the preliminaries. I ought to introduce myself."

"Oh no," Annette said. "No, you needn't bother. I would have recognised you if I'd met you in China."

He looked amused and she added swiftly, "Won't you come in first and have a sherry or something?"

"I think we ought to be off or we shall miss the start of the race. It's down at the harbour, and that's about twenty minutes' drive."

He held the car door for her, and with swift efficiency wrapped her in a rug. As he whisked the car through the narrow, twilit streets, he said, "Have you been in China?"

"Actually it was just a figure of speech, but yes, I was brought up there."

"I thought perhaps you had been."

"Do tell me why?"

"Your way of moving—and your voice. Impalpably different from those of women who have lived all their lives in the western hemisphere."

"Goodness, how fascinating," Annette said. "I wonder if it extends to one's way of thinking."

"I've hardly had an opportunity of judging that yet." He spoke gravely, but she could hear a smile in his voice, that oddly harsh, carrying voice so familiar from radio and TV. "I'll tell you in due course. Isn't the marsh wonderful in this light?"

"Wonderful."

The narrow flat road spun away before and behind them, flanked by two dykes in which gleams of water reflected the primrose-coloured evening sky. Straw-pale banks of rushes stirred in the rising offshore wind, and far away behind them the lights of Crowbridge began to twinkle out in a pyramidal shape like a Burmese temple.

"You get more varieties of light on the marsh than anywhere else in the world," he said. "If I were a yogi I'd build a hut out here and just sit and watch the light forever."

"But you couldn't just sit. You'd always be wanting to paint it."

"Yes," he said. "Yes, that's the difficulty. That's why a painter lives such a tortured existence—always dragged two ways, between the pleasure of pure observation and the need to make his own interpretation of what he observes."

The car drew up with a scrunch of tyres on shingle. They seemed to have stopped on a river-bank in the middle of nowhere but, Crispin James explained, "The road doesn't go any farther than this. We have to cross by the ferry and walk along to the harbour. Here it comes now."

Staring across the water, Annette could see the darker shape of a boat pulling out from the jetty on the other side, bobbing on the full tide. To her right the silver streak of water zigzagged across the dusk of the marsh towards Crowbridge; to her left was nothing but openness, crying of gulls, piling in of salty air with a message of tar and and old timbers and shingle and seaweed.

"Take my hand," said Crispin James, and guided her down shallow slippery steps to the water's edge, as the heavy boat bumped against a short wooden pier covered in barnacles and green weed. He nodded to the ferryman, who said, "Evenin' Mr James; haven't seen you down thisaway for dunnamany years," and then, having received their fares, returned to his oars and took no further notice of them. The boat crept slowly back across the choppy water; by the time they were in midstream the low marshy banks had disappeared entirely from view and the river seemed infinitely wide, a lagoon stretching to the world's rim. Nobody spoke in the boat; only the slop and splash of oars broke the silence, and the voices of the gulls.

But presently they began to see the lights of Crowbridge Harbour, a small huddle of houses on the sea's edge. A seawall loomed above them, and the boat scraped against a sloping ramp.

"Along the quay," Crispin James said, and guided Annette up a flight of steps and past tall, tarred warehouses smelling of malt and timber to a cobbled expanse bounded by a low stone wall. It was nearly dark now. Stars were pricking out and, looking up, Annette suddenly realised with awe that what had seemed a huge triangle of black sky above her was in fact a sail towering into the air, three times the height of a roof. Beyond it was another; out across the water, moving to and fro, were several more. . . .

"Impressive, aren't they, when you see them like that for the first time?" The warmth of a smile was in his voice again. "But it's a pity you can't see them by daylight too. They are the most wonderful dark red."

"I can hardly believe in them even now." Annette crossed to the sea-wall and looked down; below the majestic sail an occasional gleam of lantern light picked out a massive rounded poop and the solid timbering of a cabin.

There were not many spectators; a few groups here and there made inky darknesses against the dusk of the wharf. They spoke in whispers as if attending a religious ceremony, and the hushed atmosphere seemed to extend to the barges; the rare commands echoing across the water were brief and low-pitched as the five contestants, preparing for the race, slowly worked into position across the river mouth.

"They'll be a while yet before they start," Crispin James said. "Would you like to come into the Fishermen's Arms and have something to warm you?"

"Oh, thank you. But I'd rather stay here and watch, if you don't mind."

"Let's look for somewhere to sit, then," he said. They strolled farther down the quay and found a great stack of timber, all lengths and levels, which provided perching-places sheltered from the sea-wind.

"Tell me about your job," Crispin James said when he had established Annette in a comfortable niche. "Joanna said you edit another of the magazines in the group that she works for. But oughtn't you to be painting full time?"

"Oh, but I love the job," Annette said. "It's a news-magazine called *Eyewitness*—perhaps you know it? It's quite small, hasn't been going long, but you figure in its pages often enough! By your standards it must seem very crude and unfinished, but we try to make it lively."

"On the contrary," he said, "you have some excellent art-work—I'm often amazed at how you manage to achieve it in the time. I know the magazine very well. You have Rouart working for you, don't you?"

"He's not actually on the staff," Annette said, "but we use him as often as we can. He's marvellous, isn't he? He's just done us a brilliant new series called the Horrors of Spring. I'm sure they would amuse you. I'm terribly impatient to get back and see how they shape up on the page."

He asked more questions, proving himself a receptive and well-informed listener; Annette unfolded and talked with enthusiasm about her job.

"I can see why they are anxious not to lose you," Crispin James said. "They would obviously find you hard to replace. But don't you feel inclined to give it up now? I believe Joanna said something about your having come in for a legacy?

"It was a win," Annette confessed, feeling the usual shame, as if she were revealing some sordid misdemeanor. "A—a football pools win. I'd never gone in for pools before, but a form came one day in the mail—you know the kind, with the regular promotion literature. My f-father was ill at that time, in pain—I was seizing on anything that might distract him and take his mind off, so we filled it in together, more or less at random, and I posted it off and thought no more about it. Then, on the day—on the very day he died—"

She stopped, locking her fingers together, fighting for control of her voice.

Somewhere to their left a gun boomed startlingly, waking echoes among the stone-built warehouses and exciting a whole brood of sea-birds to shrill complaint. Annette took a deep breath, partly of relief, and said:

"Is that the start? Should we go back?"

"It's the five-minute gun. Yes, we might go back to the starting-line."

His voice was very kind. He took her arm and helped her carefully down from her perch.

They walked slowly back to the harbour wall.

"You can hear that the tide has turned, can't you?" Crispin James said. "It makes a different sound."

Annette nodded, forgetting for a moment that it was too dark for him to see her. She was glad of the covering dark, and of the steady, purposeful suck and swish that the hurrying water made as it raced along the quayside. Slowly in her mind the image of that unbearable day sank and faded until the anguish could once more be borne.

The gun crashed again, and a loudspeaker voice, amplified to unintelligibility, boomed out instructions. The great sails, faintly visible in line across the width of the river, turned and filled. As the last gun sounded, a faint cheer rose from the unseen spectators on the quay, of exhortation and good wishes. Then Annette heard the sound of wind in rigging, the slap of water on striving wood.

"Where is the end of the race?" she asked.

"They go round the coast and up the Thames to Gravesend—it's about eighty miles."

"How long does it take?"

"It depends on the weather and the tides. That's about all we'll see," he added after a pause, as the sails dwindled into the dark of the horizon. "Shall we go back now?"

He took her arm again and, as they strolled, asked,

"You are, aren't you, the Annette Sheldon who painted a small picture called Green Gravel that was on exhibition in Liverpool five years ago?"

"Good heavens," she said. "Yes, I am. But how ever did you come to remember it?"

"I always remember a kindred vision," he said. "I knew we should meet someday." Annette suddenly shivered and he said with concern:

"You're cold."

"No. Goose walking over my grave."

"We'll go home. I hope this won't have been bad for you."

"Oh no," she said. "It was wonderful. I wouldn't have missed it for worlds."

Noel Hanaker invited Annette out to dinner with him next evening.

She had spent the day in a curious state of expectancy, almost excitement. Prepared to find herself miserably flat and disoriented for days after two such disrupting personalities as Joanna and Philip had come and gone, she found that, on the contrary, she hardly gave them a thought. Perhaps the weather contributed to her mood: it was a dry, bright, cold, blowy day—autumn with more than a hint of winter.

In the morning sunshine her house seemed to preen itself, displaying all its charm for her benefit. Amusedly aware of this, Annette worked for a couple of hours at scraping the panels in the studio, which Joanna's Auntie Loo had chosen to paint a depressing mud-brown; she finished making-up and hung a pair of dark violet curtains and tinkered with the car, polishing it and tidying out the trunk. It pleased her that already she knew quite a few of the passers-by in the sunny cobbled street and could exchange good-mornings and hear local gossip from them. She kept a lookout for her odd neighbour Mrs Kundry, but during the whole morning nobody came or went through the creaking gate of the house next door.

"How long has Mrs Kundry been living here?" Annette

asked when Mrs Fairhall summoned her dictatorially for a glass of hot milk at noon.

"Her? Oh, donkey's years, must be well over twelve. Ever since her mum died. The daughter was living abroad then, but the house come to her, so she moved back when the funeral was over. There's no other kin in the town; Rosamund—Mrs Kundry, that is—was the only child and her dad had died previous. What became of the husband none knows—nor no one's ever set eyes on him; she got wed overseas. Her mum didn't half carry on about it, by all accounts; thought there must be something hole and corner to it, or she'd ha' brought him back for a visit. There was lots of rumours going round the town about it at the time," Mrs Fairhall said cheerfully, swishing tea-cloths through a basin of soapy water. "Some said he was a black African, others that he was a bank robber obliged to stay abroad, and my husband's auntie always swore that he was one of those Mormons and she lived in a hay-reem. Now you just get on and drink that milk while it's hot, Miss Annette dear; don't sit staring at it as if it was carbolic. Doctor's orders you're to get it down."

"I loathe milk," Annette grumbled, complying with a grin. "Mrs F, you boss me."

"Someone's got to," Mrs Fairhall said darkly.

"Would you say Mrs Kundry was a bit odd?"

"Simple, you mean?"

Annette nodded.

"She certainly does have her peculiar ways. Keeps herself to herself." Mrs Fairhall sounded detached about this failing. "Always has done from a girl. Mad about walking out on the Salts"—this was the local name for the marshes—"she's always been, rain or fine. She's not one for going to whist drives or bingo sessions. Course, she and old Miss James used to be quite thick. Old Miss James wasn't just in the common way herself; quite a character she was."

"Eccentric?"

Mrs Fairhall took a minute to think, vigorously wringing her cloths, then she said:

"Shrewd. Knew which side her bread was buttered on. For all her money, you couldn't get round her with a hardluck story. But she seemed really sorry for Rosamund Kundry, kind of took her under her wing as you might say. Kindred spirits, maybe." This was said with a sniff; did Annette gather she had had no great opinion of either of them?

"Mrs Kundry must be lonely then, now Miss James has gone."

"Lonely? Maybe so. Of course," Mrs Fairhall said dubiously, "there's always her daughter."

Annette sensed some reserve here; nevertheless, ploughing on, she said, "Her daughter? Oh, then—"

The front-door bell rang and Mrs Fairhall, hurrying to answer it—with a shade of relief?—burst into a storm of commination against the butcher's boy who, it seemed, had brought lamb chops that were only suitable to split up and use as kindling. How dared he proffer such stringy, bony, ill-favoured objects at the house of a delicate young lady who had been instructed by her doctor to eat only the very choicest cuts?

Chuckling, Annette escaped beyond range of the butcher boy's red-eared rout and returned to her wood-scraping, meditating on the luck of having acquired such a kind-hearted and redoubtable ally as Mrs Fairhall, who was plainly proposing to take personal responsibility for "Miss Annette's" total recovery in the shortest possible length of time.

During the afternoon, still trying to subdue her purposeless excitement, she decided to carry her explorations of the town a little farther, and went for a walk round the ramparts. Crowbridge was largely medieval and the town wall, high and massive, with its battlemented inner footway, was still in perfect condition and a great attraction to tourists. The rampart walk was approached up a spiral stair from the town's small museum, housed in a building known as the Dover Tower. There was no other public way on to the walls, though several houses had private footways from upper stories. The walk round the top took about three quarters of an hour, giving magnificent (as the guidebook said) views of the marsh on the seaward side of the town and the rising wooded weald to the north.

Up here the wind had a bitter bite to it, even behind the protection of the ramparts, and Annette walked briskly until she was warm, and then more slowly to admire the view. When she came to the southern point of the perimeter she stopped for a while and leaned on the parapet, looking down across the marsh, following the river's silvery zigzag to the small cluster of roofs and masts that marked the harbour where, last night, she had watched the start of the barge race with Crispin James.

It had been an unforgettable experience—really out of this world, she thought wonderingly. If anyone had suggested such a notion to me yesterday morning I would have thought it just about as likely to happen as—as taking tea with Schweitzer or a round of golf with Eisenhower.

After the race he had taken her back to the Bell, and they had drunk sloe gin in front of a roaring log fire in the oak-beamed coffee-room. They had talked about art, and Annette, usually shy and unvocal in the presence of people she revered, had found herself giving voice to her most hidden and secret ideas, talking with a fluency and verve of which she could not have believed herself capable. There seemed to be some magnetic quality in him, able to draw these things to the surface. Their talk had been exacting, fruitful, wildly stimulating, and when at last he escorted her home she felt as if her mind were full of fireworks and doubted if she would ever get to sleep.

There had been a curious episode as they said good night outside her house in Crossbow Lane: Annette, glancing up, had noticed a face staring fixedly from one of Mrs Kundry's first-floor windows—a totally white face, shocked, it seemed, into an immobility in which terror and astonishment were blended. But astonishment at what? Terror of what? Imaginary ghosts in the street at night? Some other emotion was there too, something more elusive: what was it? And was the watcher Mrs Kundry?

By the uncertain light of the dangling street-lamp it was hard to be sure. Crispen James had not noticed the incident at all.

Or could the face have been the daughter?

I am becoming a regular busybody, Annette admonished herself as she brushed her hair before getting into bed; no doubt it is a regular pattern of activity in a town like this to study the comings and goings of one's neighbours, but I'll be hanged if I let myself fall into the habit. She was probably waiting for the doctor because she had a stomach-ache. All the same, she *did* look scared, and something else too—what could it have been?

Contrary to her expectation, Annette fell asleep as soon as her head touched the pillow—fell fathoms deep into a dreamless slumber from which, in the morning, she woke feeling more rested than at any time since her illness. But just once, halfway through the night, she had found herself wide awake, staring through the dark, and had just time to think, before sleep took her again:

She was pleased. Beneath that appalled, screwed-up fright was a look of satisfaction, as if something were working out according to plan. That was it. She was pleased.

Joanna had said there were a couple of Crispin James's pictures in the little museum, and on her way down from the ramparts Annette paused to look for them.

The three round rooms in the tower housed the usual collection of trivia to be found in such places: flint arrowheads, stuffed fish caught locally, medieval utensils, engravings of the town in earlier centuries. Among these desiccated oddments the two James pictures gave an impression of startling violence and life.

They were quite extraordinarily unlike each other; if Annette, an ardent disciple and admirer of James's, had not known that like all great painters he had passed through periods of widely varying technique, she might have sworn that the canvases were by two different painters.

One, called Morning, showed a nude girl who was sitting in the foreground and looking with preoccupied attention over her shoulder at the smooth pale curve of her own back. The style was mannered: paint applied in a series of strokes and dashes; it could be felt that, though no recognisable likeness came through, the character of the sitter was interpreted with a delicacy almost amounting to satire. This picture Annette had seen before in reproductions; she had never liked it and did not now, though she was obliged in fairness to admit that it was brilliantly painted.

The other, a very characteristic James from a much later period, she had not seen before. Boldly painted in sharp strokes, the texture of the paint showing as a series of ridges, it presented a small room in the shadowed light of early morning, with a few outlines clear against a reddish sky beyond the window. Not much was visible in the room, which seemed to be an attic, irregularly shaped and sparsely furnished: a tin bath stood in the center of the floor; it was difficult to decide whether the bed in the shadows held a sleeping figure or merely a huddle of bedclothes. The whole picture was implicit with a sort of contained dramatic urgency; it seemed spellbound, breathless, as if at any minute some awaited event must take place.

Annette stood before it for a long time, half hypnotised, wondering in what lay the secret of its curious power.

"Hi there!" said a voice in her ear.

She turned dazedly, screwing up her eyes against a dusty beam of evening sun that struck sparks off the glass cases and the flint arrowheads.

"I did make a polite remark about the weather," said Noel Hanaker, "but you were lost to the world." He stood grinning at her, six feet tall and fair-haired, still in his deplorable work-clothes.

"I'm so sorry. I never heard you come in." She smiled at him apologetically.

"Admiring the works of the master? He certainly has what it takes," said Noel dispassionately. "This one's got a real flavour of Paris, hasn't it? You can almost smell the drains and the cabbages."

"Yes. Yes I suppose it has. I hadn't thought of its being Paris—I suppose that's the Sacré-Coeur you can see through the window."

"Just so." Noel took her arm and began piloting her to the door. "As for that gal"—he glanced for an instant at the second picture—"she gives me the willies."

"Oh? Why?" Annette was interested to hear this reflection of her own view.

"There's something a bit lacking about her—attitude, expression—I don't know how it's put across. Don't you see what I mean? It's damnably clever and if it's intentional it's damnably cruel—portrait of mental instability."

"I hadn't thought of that. I was trying to decide whom she reminded me of."

"If any of your friends have that look I should tactfully drop 'em," said Noel, steering her diagonally across the church square with its massive yew trees and towards Crossbow Lane. "But what I came to say was—observing you up on the ramparts as I made my grubby way home—would you honour me by coming out tonight and seeing what the Bell will do in the way of dinner?"

"It'll be pheasant or lamb or mackerel, as it's a Monday," Annette said, "and I accept with pleasure."

"Wonderful! That makes my day. I've dug up nothing since breakfast but three bits of Roman pottery, each slightly smaller than a halfpenny, and I was feeling good and downhearted. I'll go back and change these filthy rags and fetch you about seven."

"I can get to the Bell under my own steam, you know," said Annette, amused. "It's only ten minutes' walk from my house."

"Old-world courtesy, Miss Sheldon. When in Roman Britain do as Roman Britain does." He bowed deeply, hand on heart, and loped off over the cobbles.

What a nice boy, Annette thought. She supposed he must be about the same age as Philip in fact, and yet what a difference! *Boy* was the word that came naturally to mind. There was nothing complicated or concealed about him: he was direct, outgoing, yet intelligent—almost brotherly in the straightforwardness of his approach to her. Brotherly, she repeated to herself. He had said something, hadn't he, about his brother in Paris who had known Crispin James. That of course tied up with his being so familiar with the outline of the Sacré-Coeur.

And then, her mind having wandered back to Crispin James, she began speculating again about the woman in the picture and wondering when he had painted it, and whom she resembled.

Dinner at the Bell was a pleasant meal. Annette had done justice to the old-world courtesy by changing into a dress of rust-coloured chiffon which subtly underlined her black-and-white colouring. Before, Noel had felt that she was attractive, and a protective instinct in him had been called out by some vaguely forlorn, unhappy quality which he guessed at beneath her composed surface; now he suddenly realised with exhilaration that she was beautiful.

Better still, she was immediately, happily, at ease with him. Annette, indeed, finding herself blessed by a sudden exuberent rush of well-being, discovered that this was just the sort of companionship she had been wanting: somebody young, gay, unexacting, with whom she could relax. What a nice person Noel was! He said funny things about the English, but in an affectionate way, as if he found them a race of amazing old aunties. He swapped anecdotes with Annette about childhood and they found they had shared the same sordid passion for crude rhymes, drinking vinegar out of bottles, and a violent pink comic called "Spiffer" which, it seemed, had circulated in New Zealand too.

"Do you remember Plato and Tato, the Galloping Greeks?"

"And Whizzbang Willkins, the Wacky Wizard?"

"And those boys who drove a tractor down Mount Vesuvius and found a whole lot of prehistoric animals?"

"Prehistoric animals came into everything, didn't they? They must obviously represent some deep, buried urge to go back to our beginnings."

"Now you're getting in too deep for me," Noel twitted

her. "I don't dig all this social psychology stuff, down there in the Gemeinschaft."

"And do you remember those balsa-wood planes they used to give away! They always broke pretty soon but they flew marvellously."

"I've still got half a dozen at home," Noel assured her solemnly.

"Oh Noel, have you really?"

Without noticing it, they had become Noel and Annette, on comfortable teasing terms with one another. She told Noel about her job and her spare-time painting, and he told her about New Zealand. "It's a wonderful country, Annette; you really ought to come and see it. Every painter should."

"I nearly did get there once," Annette said dreamily. "My father is—was—a professor of ancient languages. He wrote books on how the way people spoke proved things about their physical make-up and which way round their spinning-wheels turned and what sort of religious beliefs they had. And we used to travel about a lot; we lived in China when I was small and he always intended to move on and live in New Zealand to study the Maori language, only then the war came, so he went and lived in the British Museum instead."

"Gay for you and your mother."

"Mother had died by then. And I was at school. But he used to emerge in the holidays and tell me wonderful things. He was really very companionable."

"Your mother wasn't English, was she?"

"No, why?" said Annette, smiling. "She was American. But *her* parents were Greek. Father used to adore old Granny Stavridi. I can just remember her. She had snow-white hair and she used to sing lovely songs—I wish I hadn't forgotten them. One of them had words that sounded like *ananyi ro,* over and over, to a sad little haunting tune; I never knew what it meant. She used to wear a tea-cosy instead of a hat, because America was so much colder than Greece."

The talk skipped to other tales of eccentric relatives,

and then Noel remarked casually, "Tell me about your friend—Miss Southley, was it? I believe I saw her in Paris a couple of months ago at an exhibition of Mexican art."

"In Paris? How queer. I didn't know she'd been. Oh, I suppose—" I suppose it was while I was in the nursing-home, she had been about to say, but bit the sentence off. "She very likely *would* be at an exhibition of Mexican art; it's just her sort of thing. Probably covering it for *Sweet Home*."

"She seems a formidable character."

"Well, yes. A bit. She's very strong-willed—and frighteningly intelligent. But great fun, very kind, once you get to know her."

"Rather like getting to know a Sherman tank?"

"Oh, come now!" But Annette was tickled at the idea; there *was* something a bit tanklike about Joanna.

"You look like a Dutch interior," Noel said irrelevantly, and Annette burst out laughing.

"Polished tiles and some fruit in a bowl? It's an original compliment if it is one!"

"Oh yes, it's a compliment." Noel was quite unabashed. "There's a kind of glow about you this evening. With all that black and white and orange—your string of amber shining in the firelight and the tangerine in your hand—please don't put it down for a moment—you know that impression of being lit up from within that some of the Dutch paintings give. . . ." He made a gesture that seemed to finish his sentence for him.

Annette was interested and leaned forward, the tangerine peel dangling from her fingers. "You know a lot about painting, don't you? Have you studied art?"

"No, but my brother did. He and I were very close, and each of us naturally absorbed a lot of what the other was doing."

"How lucky you were. I wish I'd had brothers or sisters." Now her irrepressible happiness came to the surface. "I'm going to begin again—studying painting, I mean. I'm so excited about it. Crispin James rang up this evening and suggested that I should work with him for a while. He does take young painters into his studio occasionally. Isn't it a wonderful chance?"

So this, Noel thought, was the cause of her sudden vitality and the impression she gave of having had a current switched on inside her. She was going to start painting again. With Crispin James.

He looked down at the grapes on the plate before him. They were oval and firm, green grapes covered with a bluish-silvery bloom; they lay on a blue-and-white plate. Fruit from a Dutch interior.

"You look doubtful." Annette's charming warm voice sounded puzzled. "Don't you approve? Or have you swallowed a pip?" He looked up at her and she smiled at him teasingly.

"We run-holders always swallow our pips. No, of course I think it's a grand chance for you."

And for me, perhaps, he said inwardly. Only, why did *you* have to be the one, with your warmth, and your vulnerability, and your troubling, intermittent beauty? Why couldn't it be somebody who might matter less? "You must be delighted," he said.

"Goodness, I'm thrilled!"

They picked up their coffee cups and moved into armchairs by the hearth.

"I've been rather ill, you see, and I'm supposed to vegetate for two or three months, but I loathe doing nothing. Normally I'm quite an active person but I've had a kind of convalescent depression and couldn't get going. Working with Crispin James will be just the stimulus I need. But here I am egotistically talking about myself," she broke off. "Tell me about you. And your brother. Is he still painting? Didn't you say he was in Paris?"

Noel's face changed. "He was, yes."

"And now?"

"He died," Noel said. "He died last summer."

"Oh—I'm most terribly sorry." Annette's candid eyes were dismayed. "How horribly stupid of me to chatter about painting when it's the last thing you'll want to be reminded of."

"Please don't think that. One of the reasons why I came to Europe was to try and pick up a few traces of his life before he died, for my parents' sake. That was why I wanted to see Crispin James. I think I mentioned Robin had worked with him a bit in Paris?"

"*Did* he? I see. Did Crispin James tell you much about him?"

"Well, no. Not a lot." Noel looked vaguely troubled. "I just missed seeing him—Mr James—in Paris, and by the time I caught up with him here he—he seemed to have pretty well forgotten about Rob—didn't have much to tell me really. It was rather disappointing, because I'd gathered he was something of a hero to Rob, who just about worshipped the ground he trod on."

"Rob was younger than you?"

"Three years. He was rather a wild kid—what you'd call a beatnik, I suppose," Noel said with a half smile. "My father wanted him to study law, but he was never interested in anything but painting, and when he finished school he had a row with my parents and left home. Presently we heard he'd worked his passage to Europe in a cattle-boat. They had no letters from him but he did write to me and Jill, that's my sister, every so often. At first his letters from Paris were wildly enthusiastic, then after a few months something seemed to go wrong. Reading between the lines, I gathered he'd taken to drink pretty heavily—he had a series of part-time jobs but they always folded up sooner or later."

"What about his painting?"

"That was the queer part. He was pretty good—there was no doubt that he had a lot of talent. His professors at home said so, and he told me Crispin James did too. But after he'd been in Paris about nine months his inspiration—ideas, creative ability, whatever you call it—seemed to dry up. His letters to me became frantic; he said he was doing bad work, nothing worth keeping . . ."

"And?"

"And in the end he took an overdose of sleeping-tablets."

"Oh, dear God," Annette said. "I'm *sorry*. If I'd known—"

"How could you? Don't, please, worry about it. It's over now. He was never a very well-balanced person. He could easily fall into a state of utter despair about what he was doing. He was a nice kid, though," Noel said simply.

"What about his paintings? Did you get them when you went to Paris?"

"There were very few," Noel said. "I think he must have been destroying them as fast he he produced them."

"What were they like?"

"Horrifying," he said slowly. "Messy daubs, that might have been painted by a backward child. He must have had a complete mental breakdown."

"Oh, Noel—how dreadful for you." The complete sincerity and pity in her eyes was an unexpected blow to his self-control. He wanted to spring to his feet and warn her, tell her at all costs to move away, sell her house and go back to London, to her safe, distracting job—

"But what a very great pleasure."

They both looked up quickly at the unexpected voice. Crispin James was standing in the doorway, smiling at them. In a velvet smoking-jacket he looked like a nineteenth-century elder statesman, elegant, urbane, and startlingly impressive with his deep-set luminous eyes and silvering hair. "Mr Hanaker—and my new pupil. How delightful! I just dropped in for some cigarettes. Won't you both come back to my house for a drink? My spendthrift cousin Joanna brought me a bottle of slivovitz."

Before Noel could say that he was too busy, that he had to be early on the site tomorrow, that they were going to the cinema, that he was just about to take Annette for a moonlight walk on the ramparts, she was on her feet.

"Mr James, how nice of you. We'd love to—I'm longing to see your studio. May I? I haven't been in it yet."

"Of course you may, my dear. I hope that tomorrow you'll be working in it."

"I can't wait to get started."

Her eyes were shining. Noel, helping her into her corduroy coat, suddenly felt as if it weighed a thousand pounds.

Annette woke in the middle of the night; she was too happy and stimulated to stay asleep. She lay relaxed, her arms behind her head, her mind racing in top gear. What a splendid evening it had been! What a wonderful, fascinating personality Crispin James was, and how could she ever appreciate her incredible luck in having him for a neighbour, living in this enchanted town, starting to paint again seriously.

She had been a fool to let that unreasonable depression weigh her down. Now she could hardly believe that it had existed; it seemed to have drifted away like a black cloud. Death was dreadful; but it must be faced and accepted, even the death of a loved relative. Noel's brother had died and he was facing the fact, not taking refuge in nervous illness; Noel was calm and well-balanced, and so would she be. As for the money and the office—she found it difficult even to remember that she had been unhappy about that burden, worried about getting back to her job; now all that seemed very far away and unimportant.

At some point during the evening in Crispin James's house they had been discussing portrait painting, and the subject of personality had come up.

"Actually there is no such thing as personality," James pronounced. "We are all merely the sum of our actions, and as our actions are widely varied, at any given minute we are the sum of the actions we represent just then."

"So we are really just a collection of memories?" Annette said.

"Of course. And as our memories are linked together in chains, we are the product of the particular chain to which present circumstances have given a tug. Or perhaps I should say circuits—something touches a switch in you, contact is made, a series of memories comes to mind and—click—you are the personality that those memories represent in you."

"But one set must be more important than another,"

Noel suggested. "After all, most people's personalities have a definite twist one way or another."

"Oh, certainly. But the dominant layer need not be apparent. That is why I seldom paint portraits, and only if I know the subject very well. How can one be sure that one has really hit on the—the—"

"The winning series?" Noel grinned at his host.

"I think that's a frightening theory," Annette said. "It means that all our different layers are quite separate and there's no central control—it's like being on lots of different roller-skates that are all running away in different directions."

"Oh, not necessarily." Crispin James smiled at her, but the expression in his eyes was disturbingly penetrating. "So long as your memories are accessible to you, the control of all your personalities is in your own hands."

Then he had changed the subject by showing them some wonderful Japanese flower paintings and the talk had strayed elsewhere. Noel asked if his brother had done any flower-painting while he was working with Crispin James in Paris. "He used to be rather good at them at home; a publisher offered him a contract for a book on New Zealand flora, but he turned it down."

A faint cloud came over Crispin James's face. "No, your brother did no flower paintings when he was with me," he answered curtly. "In any case, I should have been little use to him; flower-painting is not my metier. But, as I told you, the time he spent working with me was very brief; he may well have done work that I did not see."

Noel asked one or two more questions, but Crispin James's replies became briefer still; the memory of Noel's brother appeared to be somehow disagreeable to him. Annette's attention wandered back to his last remark about personality. Could it be true? Or was it only a theory? Supposing all one's memories were not accessible? What would happen to one's personality then?

Glancing at her watch, she rose briskly and declared that if she was to do any decent work the next day, she must now go home to bed.

Noel walked her home through the windy moonshine along the short cobbled streets that lay between her house and Crispin James's. She was dazzled, silent, overwhelmed with the number of new impressions she had received in the course of the last few days.

Noel, uncharacteristically, was silent too, but there was no discomfort about it; nice boy, he had not seemed to mind a bit when Crispin James took over their evening. At Annette's door, relinquishing her elbow, he said, "Annette, you look so fetching in the moonshine that it seems downright ungallant not to kiss you and start a series of beautiful memories, but I don't think now is the time, do you?"

Annette, smiling at him, still bemused, said, "Noel, what a sweet person you are," and he had ruffled her dark hair in a comradely way, said, "Go get some sleep," and swung off down the street.

A wonderful evening. Nonetheless, Annette wished that the topic of memory had not come up. The doctor had told her not to worry about her temporary blackouts, but it was horrible to feel that part of oneself was not—what word had Crispin James used? Accessible, that was it. Horrible to feel part of oneself was not accessible. Supposing, someday, she forgot something really important. Dr Whitney had said that in Crowbridge there was nothing important to forget, but just the same—supposing she did?

She had been stretched on her back, her eyes fixed absently on a light that was playing over her ceiling. It was like the reflection of headlights from the street, but now it occurred to her that of course it could not be headlights, since the street was on the other side of the house. Could someone be in her garden with a light? At this time of night?

She got up and looked out of the window. Somebody *was* in the garden, on the lawn, moving about with a torch, shining it here and there, now down, now up. The moon had set and the night was quite dark; she could not see who the intruder was. She flung open the window and indignantly called:

"Hi! Who are you? What do you think you're doing?"

Instantly the light was switched off. The normal silence and dark of 3 A.M. lay over the garden.

Annette hesitated. Should she go down and investigate? It hardly seemed worth while—whoever it was would be well away by the time she had put on shoes and coat and unlocked the door.

In the end she returned to bed, read for an hour, lay wakeful for another, and fell asleep just as the first grey of day was beginning to show over the marsh.

IV

"I want you to draw circles," Crispin James said. "Nothing but circles until your wrist is loose. We are starting at the beginning, you see; I am pretending I know nothing about your work. And as for you, your painting eye has been asleep, your painting hand is stiff; we must get you flexible and at ease before we start to build. Circles, then: in paint, charcoal, Indian ink, what your prefer."

He had tacked large sheets of cartridge paper on one wall of his studio and, as Annette picked up a paintbrush and began obediently describing circles in scarlet paint, he walked over to the window and continued to talk.

"Do them at all levels. Fill the paper completely.

"You can learn a lot about a civilisation from the level that its folk art has reached. And when I say level I mean it literally: eye-level, waist-level, knee-level. Art at eye-level is the most primitive—if a child draws on a wall he does it at the height of his own eye. It takes a sophisticated culture to create art in its ceilings, in its footwear.

"Draw as fast as you can—circle after circle, large and small. Let your wrist loosen.

"Where is the folk art of our own civilisation? It hardly exists. But there are occasional manifestations. Teacloths, for instance. Eye-level, you see—very primitive. And record-sleeves. A little more sophisticated—knee-level perhaps."

"Table-mats?" Annette suggested.

"A few, perhaps. But most of them are not folk-art so much as pseudo-culture. Continue with your circles—I am only talking nonsense in order to get you to relax."

Annette went on with her circles while he drew an ingenious parallel between teacloths and the Bayeux tapestry, between the pictures on cereal packets and those on Byzantine mosaics.

"The essential in art," he pronounced, "—the Byzantines knew this—is to be aware of what you are doing. You must be fully in control."

"You don't approve of throwing paint at the canvas and then riding a bicycle over it?" Annette said, laughing. "Though even then if you have the brakes on I suppose you are in control to some extent."

Crispin James looked disapproving. "Childish antics," he said. "Fit only for five-year-olds and mental defectives. If you don't control your work it is because you can't, and if you can't, you should be under sedatives, or having shock treatment, away from normal people."

Annette was curious. "Mr James," she said, "you remember Noel's brother—did you know he had a mental breakdown?"

His face darkened. "I prefer not to talk about it, but—yes. The seeds of his collapse must have been in him from birth, poor creature; he was hopelessly unstable. In the end he became quite unhinged. A hateful deterioration. There was no point in describing it to his brother."

"I see," Annette said slowly. "How dreadful. Poor Noel. Yes, it's as well as he shouldn't hear all the details."

"Particularly as I should imagine it might well be congenital." Crispin James's tone was dry. "Insanity is the most unbearable human affliction—nobody wants to feel it may be in store for him.—But let us leave this abominable subject. Tell me about your father—now there was a happy example of a brilliant brain, perfectly in control of its subject. I have many of his books."

He led Annette on to talk of her father, which she did gladly. And presently, by gentle, sympathetic, persistent questioning, he even drew from her the story of those last agonising weeks when Professor Sheldon had been dying of a painful and incurable disease.

"It—it was so *undignified* for him," Annette brought out, with tears in her eyes—but she found the horror diminished to bearable proportions now it had been faced and shared. "It just seemed intolerable that a man of his intelligence and integrity, with so much work still to do, should have to go through such a disgusting ordeal and die. But he bore it. He bore it better than I did."

"It may seem terrible to you," Crispin James said, "but however painful his ordeal was, however terrible, think how much better it is to die at the height of one's powers, knowing one still has the ability to do good work, than to outlive one's capacity and dwindle into senile impotence. Your father was lucky in that respect."

He spoke with such passion that Annette looked at him wonderingly. Surely such a state could have no application to him? Catching her look, he gave her a wry smile.

"I'm sorry," he said. "Mental deterioration is a bugbear of mine—I didn't mean to return to the subject. But believe me, there might have been worse ends than that of your father. And at least he had a beloved daughter to help him endure it."

The smile he gave her was so warmly approving that Annette blushed pink and bent her head over her paintpot.

The studio was very warm. It was a big upstairs room with windows at both ends which could be curtained to exclude direct light but which were now letting in the full flood of autumn sunshine. There was a soothing smell of wood and canvas, paint and linseed; stacks of canvases lay and leaned in most of the available space. Every now and then, as Annette moved, her eye was caught by some tantalising fragment of colour or detail of a painting. She longed to stop and look. But there would be time, plenty of time. . . . There was all the time in the world. . . .

The Crowbridge *Recorder and Southern Bulletin* was housed in a diminutive Tudor cottage in the High Street, between the remains of a monastery and the shocking red-and-gold façade of a cut-price store which had somehow won its way in against the anguished protest of half the town's residents and to the delighted acclamations of the other half.

Noel strolled into the little front office, which was papered round with curling sepia prints of bygone weddings.

"Hullo chick," he said to the buxom sixteen-year-old at the desk. "Haven't they sent you out on a story yet? Never mind, someone's bound to fall out of bed and slip a disc sooner or later. Is Mr Barabbas in?"

"I'll see," the girl said, unwrapping her legs from the legs of her chair and dropping a copy of *Teens Toons* on the floor.

This was a pure formality, as Noel knew; old Mr Barabbas never went out. He spent his days doing crossword puzzles and working out chess problems in the upstairs room; when a story broke (if such a decisive word could be used for Crowbridge news) he sent out a young man who at other times kept the filing system up to date or ran off agendas of town council meetings and announcements of bingo sessions.

"Mr Hanaker? Couldn't have come at a better moment. Come in, come in! What do you make of this: 'Irish nineteenth-century cops'? No, 'domestic utensils'! Two words . . . six, seven. Can't be Bow Street Runners."

"Potato peelers," Noel said without an instant's thought. "May I have a look at your files, Mr Barabbas?"

"Of course, my dear boy; help yourself. You know the way. Somers is out, covering a burst water main. With his cloak, no doubt. 'Through all the [something] scenes of life,' what can that be, now?"

Noel ducked under a five-foot doorway into a long low dim room that extended over the premises next door (it had at one time been the monastery's dormitory). Now it housed files and bound volumes of the Crowbridge *Recorder* back to the year 1790. Noel pulled open the drawer of a sternly modern steel filing-cabinet and hunted for JAMES, Crispin. He found his quarry without difficulty: three fat folders, stuffed with the history of awards, presentations, speeches, decorations, reviews of exhibitions. . . . Doggedly he ploughed through clipping after clipping.

"Finding what you want?" Mr Barabbas called presently, solving a final clue and preparing to move on to a fresh puzzle.

"Not yet. Trouble is, I don't really quite know what I am looking for." Something odd, he thought, something uncharacteristic, something awry in the glossy pattern of honours and success.

But nothing of the kind seemed to be in evidence, though Noel lingered doubtfully over a clipping that announced that a Mrs G Benenden of Crossbow Lane had presented an early Crispin James painting to the town museum. Why had Mrs Benenden been so generous? Noel wondered. If she had hung on to the picture it would be worth a handsome sum by now. Perhaps she had taken a dislike to it. He could share her feelings. He hunted in the files under B and found more references to the Benenden family, a numerous clan, but no more acts of altruism on the part of Mrs G, who had died of pneumonia fifteen years before, leaving a small estate to her only daughter. Not a rich woman, then.

Sighing, Noel returned the folders to their places.

"No luck?" Mr Barabbas looked up over his rimless glasses. "Eh, dear, six o'clock already, time to shut up shop. Well, come along my boy, you can keep me company in an old and mild at the Fighting Cocks. How are those diggings of yours getting on? Got another news story for us yet?"

"Nothing special," Noel said absently. "Tell me, is there a decent electronics equipment store in the town?"

"Electronics?" Mr Barabbas stared at him. "You ain't one of these fellers who believe you can pick up reverberations of Roman remarks out of the ether, are you?"

"No, sir." Noel grinned. "Just strictly contemporary stuff."

"Well, there's Jessel's, Mr Barabbas said doubtfully, "but they haven't got much beyond the cat's whisker. You'd be better advised to go over to Broadsea."

Thursdays were market days in Crowbridge, and on a Thursday afternoon Noel Hanaker ran across Annette in the market place. He was buying cheap tough dungarees, and she, rather absent-mindedly, was laying in shrubs for her garden.

The market contained everything—produce, ironmongery, livestock, secondhand books, glass jewellery and clothespegs sold by gypsies, worthy-looking cakes and jams sold by members of the Women's Institute.

"This is a fruity old English scene," Noel said with relish, taking Annette's basket. "Looks like a colour photograph straight out of a travel magazine. All you want is a few Beefeaters and Chelsea Pensioners. Only thing I don't like is the stock cooped up in those tiny pens. Do you suppose the crime rate would fall if they made it compulsory for every citizen to walk through a prison once a year? Seeing things shut up gives me the willies."

"I daresay it would," said Annette vaguely. She was bemused by the colour and noise, the shouts, barking and bleating, the smells of cattle and chrysanthemums and tractor-oil. Noel gave her a sharp look.

"How's the painting going? Are you hard at work?"

"Oh, yes!" She spoke vigorously, but then her eyes wandered back to the banked and fiery masses of dahlias on a stall; she gave the impression of being hardly conscious that Noel was there. She was rather pale and her eyes were unusually bright.

"Needn't have asked, need I?" Noel said. "What are you working on?"

"Oh—" she brought her eyes back to his like a good child reminded by the teacher. "I'm doing a study of the marsh, in oils, on my own, part of the time—Mr James lets me do that without interfering—and a whole series of quick impressions, some water-colour, some oil, under his tuition. He picks the subject and advises me; often we drive round the country and find a spot. I never thought I could learn such a lot so fast . . ." her voice trailed off.

"I'd love to see your paintings sometime," Noel said, recalling her attention once more.

"Oh—oh yes. When they're all finished." She smiled at him dreamily and began to walk away. "I must take these plants home and then go back to the studio for a couple of hours."

"I hoped you could come and have some tea at the Copper Kettle."

"I really ought to work," she said doubtfully. "There's such a lot I want to do."

"An hour off won't hurt. Be good for you." Noel's eyes on her were intent, and rather anxious.

"Well, perhaps . . ."

They crossed the crowded market, Annette hurrying ahead, hardly troubling to see if Noel was behind her. Suddenly, at an intersection, she paused.

"Remembered something you wanted?" He caught up with her.

"No—no, it's not that. I just thought I saw—" She stared in a puzzled manner at a wheel-chair which a girl was pushing slowly in front of a line of stalls. Its occupant was an elderly man, his crippled legs wrapped in a rug.

"Someone you know?"

"No—I don't know. Something reminded me . . ." She shook her head again perplexedly and turned up the steep cobbled street that led to the upper town. Noel followed her, frowning.

The Copper Kettle was two steps down from the street, and darkish, crammed full of little gate-legged oak tables set too close together. It had a powerful smell of soda scones and raffia mats.

"Every time I come in here," said Noel, "I expect to knock half a dozen china plates off the walls. Why do they hang them up there, do you suppose?"

"You ought to be thankful for them. If it weren't nice willow-pattern plates it would be poker-work pictures of ladies in crinolines with hollyhocks. Do you come here often, then?"

"I'm learning to understand the English passion for tea," Noel explained. "By four o'clock in the afternoon you need something hot and sustaining to ward off the rheumatic chills."

"But I thought all—all Antipodeans *lived* on tea?"

"You were going to say colonials," he accused her. "Weren't you?"

Annette chuckled. "Tea and *dampers*—whatever they are. And tomato ketchup."

Her eyes were brighter. A tinge of colour had come into her pale cheeks.

Noel called for their bill. "Hurry up," he said; "swig down the last of that brackish brew. I'm going to take you out for a quick run to see my villa."

"Oh, Noel. Really I don't know if I have time."

"Of course you have time," he told her, shepherding her down the alley that led from the High Street to the Bell's constricted little car park. "You won't do yourself any good if you paint till you're in a state of collapse. Clamber in, now. You have to give that door a mighty bang and then wind that piece of string round the heater knob to keep the door from coming open again."

"This is practically kidnapping."

"High time, too. It's nearly three weeks since I started trying to get you to come and see the villa—the old boy keeps your nose too close to the grindstone."

"Oh, but I love it."

"It's unsuitable diet for a convalescent."

"Have you had any exciting finds at your villa lately?" she asked politely.

He grinned. "You're trying to change the subject, but I'll let you. The most valuable thing we found was a gold ring; that's gone off to the National Museum, but presently we're going to have a local exhibition of all the finds and you can see it then. And there's a very nice jug with hounds and hares on it—I'll show you that; it's back at the Bell. And some bits of glass."

"Is it a big villa?"

"Not very. Seaside place, probably." He shuddered. "Brrr—think how the poor devils must have suffered from the cold. It's just off the marsh, which was all covered by sea then, on a sort of hilly peninsula. Here we are."

The road had been climbing; they had left the flat, dun-coloured levels of marsh behind, and now he swerved his car abruptly through a gate into a hummocky field and pulled up by a series of trenches covered with tarpaulins.

Annette got out of the car reluctantly, shivering. She was fairly indifferent to Roman remains; so far as she was concerned they could continue to remain forever undisturbed.

But to her surprise she found that Noel's enthusiasm infused unexpected interest into the site.

"Aren't they *complete*," she said, fascinated by a whole section studded with upright chimneys, which he told her was the heating-chamber. "Imagine their being here just like this for two thousand years and nobody knew."

"Oh well, some of them had fallen down, of course, but we put them up again. All this was buried about six feet deep. Then here are the heating ducts that led to the other part of the villa. Here's a bit of mosaic—rather dull, I'm afraid, but the eye of faith can just detect the head of a boy. This was the bath house and this was probably stables. Here we found a heap of junk which was probably the kitchen midden—masses and masses of broken pots and oyster shells. They must just about have lived on oysters—from Colchester or Whitstable, I daresay."

"How extraordinary." Annette sifted through the heap of shells. "Well, I suppose it's a decenter form of rubbish than rusty cans and plastic squeezers. May I have a shell to keep?"

"Sure. Have a dozen. And some bits of pot. Be my guest. What'll you do with them?"

"Paint a picture of them, maybe. Composition with oystershells."

"Well, as you do so, spare a thought for those poor shivering Romans sucking down oysters while they sat with their feet on the hot pipes."

"Noel, I really ought to get back now," Annette said, glancing at her watch.

He was disappointed. "I hoped you'd come to dinner at the Bell and admire my jug."

"Another time. For one thing, I've still got those plants to put in."

"Oh well," he sighed, "at least that's healthy outdoor exercise." He slammed the battered car door.

"Honestly," she said, laughing as they sped back towards Crowbridge, "you fuss over me even more than Mrs Fairhall does."

"You shouldn't look so fragile and blossom-like. Which evening will you be free to have dinner and admire the jug?"

"Oh, Noel—it's sweet of you, but can I let you know? I'd like to see it—it sounds lovely—but I really am awfully busy. But thank you for the tea and the ride today; I did enjoy it. . . ." She smiled at him vaguely. Almost before he had pulled up outside the house in Crossbow Lane she opened the car door, her spirit already flying ahead to her studio. She gave Noel a preoccupied wave, her gaze just brushing his, and hurried into her house.

Noel stared at the closed door for several minutes after she had gone inside. His brow was creased with worry. And presently, having discovered the limitations of Jessel's Telly Corner Shop, he got out the car again and drove swiftly over to Broadsea.

Annette ran down to the bottom of her garden, intending to leave her plants in a bucket of water overnight. Threading the little path through the bamboo clump in front of the greenhouse, she came unexpectedly face to face with the woman from next door, Mrs Kundry.

They were almost equally embarrassed.

"Oh, Miss Sheldon, I'm sure you won't know what to think," the little woman said in a breathless, flustered whisper, pushing back strands of wispy grey hair from her forehead. "Do please excuse, but I didn't mean any harm. I was just—"

"It's perfectly all right," Annette reassured her.

"It was just—Miss James used to let me pick a few herbs in her back garden, she had such lovely ones—and, do you know, for a minute I quite forgot she wasn't here any longer. I just slipped in for a bit of chervil."

She was plaiting her fingers nervously together and her eyes flickered away from Annette's face down to the path at their feet.

"Of course," Annette said quickly. "Take as much as you want. There are lots of herbs in the bed. Don't bother to ask—just come and help yourself whenever you like."

"Oh, thank you, Miss Sheldon; that is kind of you. Miss James was just the same, always kind. Some people used to be nervous of her, she had such a sharp way with her, but she was a real friend to me."

"You must miss her very much," Annette said.

"Oh I do! Every day! Do you know"—Mrs Kundry's beseeching gaze reminded Annette of a begging dog—"I'm not very well off, you see—I just have the house and my tiny bit of income which is hardly sufficient to cover the repairs and outgoings and never leaves me enough for any small comforts—so Miss James used to have a little joke: she used to say, 'I'm leaving a pot-plant for you, Rosie, on the shelf in the greenhouse. Water it and it will be sure to grow,' and, do you know, inside the flowerpot she always used to tuck a—a pound note. Wasn't that kind of her?"

"It was indeed," said Annette, thinking that it also sounded very unlike Joanna's tales of her Auntie Loo, and threw quite a new light on the old lady's character. "They are a kind family altogether, aren't they?" Some instinct had prompted Annette not to discuss Crispin James with Noel, in whom she sensed reservations, but to Mrs Kundry she could not resist adding, "Miss James's cousin is very kind too, isn't he? Mr Crispin James. He's teaching me to paint; he's being wonderful to me."

Mrs Kundry looked at her blankly, and Annette suddenly felt a fool, chattering like a rave-struck schoolgirl. She blushed, and added, "I must go and do some work now, Mrs Kundry, but do take all the herbs you want any time. Goodbye."

As she crossed the lawn towards the house, something that glittered caught her eye among the roots of a tall clump of feathery Michaelmas daisies.

She picked it up. It was a child's humming-top made of

brightly painted tin. She stared at it in bewilderment for a moment. No children had been in her garden since she moved in. Where had the top come from? It had not been there yesterday, she was sure. Could it belong to Mrs Kundry? What an enigma the little woman was with her odd fits and starts of nervousness, and her faintly forlorn, uncared-for air; Annette felt guiltily that she ought to take more interest in her neighbour, try and be a substitute for the departed Miss James, but she had so much else to think about! And there was something about Mrs Kundry that left her feeling vaguely ill at ease—an off-key quality, hard to pin down. Rather shamefacedly Annette took a pound note from her purse, ran back to the greenhouse, and tucked the note into a clean flowerpot where it could not fail to be seen. Then, returning to the house, she hurried up to her studio and at once forgot Noel, Mrs Kundry, her plants, and the mysterious top as if they had been wiped off the surface of her mind.

Annette painted steadily all the next morning, deaf to Mrs Fairhall's suggestions that she should go out and get a bit of fresh air. It was not until noon that, with a conscience-stricken start, she remembered the plants she had bought the previous day.

Sighing, she put down her brush and pulled on the thick sweater that she wore for gardening.

While she painted the sky had become overcast: it was chill, grey, and gloomy. Her garden suddenly looked unfriendly, reproaching her for neglect: the lawn needed mowing, dead rose-heads drooped, shedding brown petals; rusty leaves fluttered from the giant pear-tree that grew against the rampart wall at the end of the garden. No birds sang.

I must ask Fairhall if he can come twice a week instead of only once, Annette thought, shivering; forgetting that, at the start, she had almost decided to dispense with his services entirely. She pushed open the greenhouse door and stopped short in dismay and astonishment. The shrubs which she had left with their roots soaking in a bucket of water had been dragged out, scattered about, trampled and broken, as if in some senseless, childish prank.

But the pound note was gone.

Annette was still digesting this scene, utterly at a loss, when she heard voices calling from the house.

"Yoo-hoo! Anybody about? May we come through into the garden?"

Two figures appeared from the french window, the plump, smaller one running ahead, the lanky one hesitantly in the rear.

"Miss Sheldon? We didn't gate-crash, honestly—we rang at the bell and your housekeeper said you were out here. Are we butting in? Are you collecting inspiration? If so, say the word and we'll go away."

"Tilly! How lovely to see you! No, of course you're not butting in; I'm perfectly delighted. Are you on holiday? How is it you're gadding about the countryside on a Friday?"

"Oh well, you see, I just got engaged," Tilly said offhandedly. She dragged forward the young man who was lurking behind her. "This is Patrick. Isn't he a beanpole? But we seem to hit it off. His family live at Broadsea, so I wangled an extra day from Sourpuss Southley so we could come down to see them, and then I thought, why not call in on you on our way? It's time someone from the office came to see how you were getting on. You still don't look quite the thing, if you don't mind my saying so, does she, Patrick?"

"It's a bit hard for me to say, considering I've never met her before," Patrick murmured diffidently. He gave Annette a shy, engaging grin.

"Calling in was a wonderful idea," Annette said warmly. "Come into the house and have a drink and tell me all the gossip."

"I'm dying to see the house; I heard Miss Southley describing it to the managing director—of course she wouldn't demean herself to speak of it to *me*. It sounded luscious. I say, Patrick, isn't this fab—shall we have our house like it when we're married? Dig the shell-shaped mirrors; I bet you didn't find those growing on trees! Miss Sheldon, you are a lucky girl!"

Annette showed them all over the house and Tilly followed chattering irrepressibly, exclaiming in admiration, exhorting Patrick to take note of everything.

"It honestly is just like a *film*-star's place," she said artlessly, as they returned to the sitting-room and Annette poured drinks. "I'll bet you won't want to come back to the office after this."

"Oh, but I do. I'm longing to." Handing salted nuts, though, Annette suddenly wondered if this was entirely true—as true, anyway, as it would have been two weeks ago?

"Well, I can tell you, we're longing to have you back. Patrick, honey, I've left my cigarettes in Hereward—be a saint and fetch them. Honestly, Miss Sheldon," Tilly went on, leaning forward earnestly, "I hate to use strong language in front of my fiancé, but it's just *hell* without you; Miss Southley is a prize bitch if ever there was one."

Annette couldn't help laughing, Tilly's words were so totally at odds with her appearance. At just nineteen she was easily the most efficient secretary Annette had ever had: a round, roly-poly dumpling of a girl with a solemn expression, a lively tongue, a strong sense of moral values, and no respect for anybody, from the managing director downwards, unless he came up to her exacting standards.

She went on now, round-eyed:

"She makes Harris come in at *half-past nine!* Can you imagine it? *Harris!* I doubt if he's ever got *up* at half-past nine in his life before. Kate pointed out that most days he doesn't leave the office till half-past nine at night, and Miss Southley just said he must learn to adjust his life to normal procedure."

"Oh, lord," Annette groaned. "What about poor Kate? Is she bearing up?"

"She looks kind of harried all the time. Miss Southley conducted an awful inquisition into the stock books and the amounts paid for all the items, and the amount of bought overmatter—I heard them going on for hours. And when Kate came out she was quite *white*. Oh, thank you, sugarpie—cigarette, Miss Sheldon?"

"Do make it Annette, won't you?" Annette said, accepting one.

Tilly blushed with pleasure. "May I?—I'd love to. Well, then there was a terrible row with the Feature Department because that—because Miss Southley said she'd got to see everything before it was passed. You can think of the time that's wasted, going to and fro! Yes, thank you, I'd love another nut. I ought to think of my figure but I'll forget it just this once."

"She says that every time," Patrick put in.

"You hush up! But the worst row," Tilly went on, her large grey-green kitten's eyes wide with horror at the recollection, "was with Rouart."

"Rouart? How did he—?"

"It was over that series he did—the Horrors of Spring. Well, when Miss Southley passed it over to *Sweet Home* he was so angry that he said he'd never *ever* do another thing for—"

"What?" Annette could not believe her ears. "She passed that series over to *Sweet*— You're not serious?"

"Oh yes. Didn't you know? The first one's out already. Harris was so furious he complained to the managing director, but he just said he had every confidence in Miss Southley. So then Harris said he'd resign, but we all begged him not to and said it wasn't fair to you, and we managed to persuade him. Gosh, Miss Sh—Annette, are you all right? You do look wan, all of a sudden."

"All your chat's giving her a headache, I shouldn't wonder," remonstrated Patrick. "Shall we go away and leave you in peace, Miss Sheldon?"

"No, I'm all right, thanks," Annette said, and sipped her drink. "It was just a bit of a shock hearing about the series. But tell me about your own news. When are you going to be married?"

"Oh, not for centuries. Kildare here has to qualify first. And after that he does a year as house physician and all that jazz." Tilly rattled on cheerfully and Annette listened and asked questions. The talk did not return to the *Eye-witness* office until at last Tilly fixed her large eyes accusingly on Annette and said, "You *are* looking tired. Patrick, why didn't you drag me away before I talked her to death? Come on, we must be hitting the road."

"No, do stay to lunch, won't you?" Annette said mechanically.

"Honestly, thanks, we mustn't. Patrick's mother is expecting us."

Patrick said gruffly, "Thanks for the fine drinks. I wonder if—?"

"He wants you to come and see his car," Tilly diagnosed. "We left her at the end of the street because of the cobbles. Can you walk that far?—But not if you're tired."

"Of course I can."

Annette accompanied them to the end of Crossbow Lane and duly admired Patrick's car, an immense, slightly patched, but stately Rolls.

"We call him Hereward because he looks like a Wake. All we want is a black plume or two—and don't I wish it was Miss Southley's coffin in the back," Tilly added with sudden ferocity. "Honestly, Miss Sh—Annette, *do* get better soon. We miss you *terribly.*"

She hung out of the venerable car waving and blowing kisses as Hereward rolled imposingly away.

Annette stood looking after them as long as the car could be seen; then she shivered suddenly and uncontrollably, pressing the backs of her hands against her eyes. She stood for a moment or two thus, with her head bent, swaying slightly; then opened her eyes and shook her head to clear it.

Distantly she heard the voices of a man and a little girl going by.

"Daddy, what shall I do with my lolly stick?"

"We'll go on a little way and perhaps we'll find a litter bin."

They went on. Had she imagined curiosity and concern in the man's face as he passed her? She stared about her dazedly. Why had she come out? What was it she had meant to do?

"Hi there," said a voice behind her. She turned and saw Noel making his way over the cobbles.

"What are you doing here?" he said, "alone and palely loitering on the cold hill's side? Come along, it's nippy without a coat, you should be indoors." He tucked an arm through hers and strolled with her towards her house, talking easily. "I was proposing to come and inveigle—good word, eh?—inveigle you round to the Bell for a steak lunch, but you look whacked, as if you should be in bed with hot soup and a murder mystery. Been having tiresome company?"

"Company? I—no, I don't think so," Annette answered in a vague tone, letting him steer her through her front door and into the sitting-room. Glasses and littered ashtrays stood about. She gave them a puzzled glance, looked up to meet Noel's anxious, searching eyes, and said nervously:

"Oh, Noel, do go away. Please. Don't stay just now. I'm really most terribly tired."

With a harassed gesture she pressed her fingers to her forehead again and repeated, "Please go."

"All right," Noel said slowly. "I won't bother you. But you'll go to bed, will you?"

"Yes—all right—maybe. Thank you. I'll see."

She wasn't listening to her own words; she was willing him to leave. He started to speak, thought better of it and, giving her a last troubled glance, finally backed into the hall. She heard the front door slam behind him.

V

Annette waited five minutes after Noel had gone: motionless, in the same position. Then, moving slowly but steadily as if she had come to a decision after profound thought, she went upstairs, took off her gardening sweater, and collected a portfolio from her studio. She ran down the stairs again, let herself quietly out of the front door, and, after glancing quickly up and down the street to make sure Noel was out of sight, set off with a feeling of liberation and joy for Crispin James's house, five minutes' walk away on the south side of the town.

He had built himself a large studio at the side of his house. It had two entrances, one internal, one from the street up a flight of steps, and ran the whole length of his garden, which, like Annette's, was bounded by the high town wall. A further flight of steps led on up to the rampart walk, while the studio's big south window, a recent addition, pierced clean through the town wall.

Crispin James had given Annette a key, though the staircase door generally stood open. A tiny vestibule lay inside, with another door leading to the house, and beyond it the studio itself.

Crispin James was there, working on a nearly completed study of nets and gulls. He greeted her with pleasant formality.

"Ah, Annette my dear. How delightful to see you."

"I couldn't keep away," Annette said, smiling at him. She walked round to the picture she was working on and gave it a long, careful survey.

"But you look a little tense," he said. "Has something

disturbed you? What have you been doing with yourself for the last two days? I've hardly seen you."

"Oh, I bought some plants in the market yesterday. Mr. Hanaker was there—Noel."

"Ah yes, the bearded young digger. What did he have to say?"

Annette racked her brain to remember. "I wasn't paying much attention, I'm afraid. I was thinking about this picture." He smiled indulgently. "Oh yes—he took me to see his Roman villa. And asked when he could see my work."

"And you said?"

"When I had enough pictures for a show."

"Very sensible." His tone was approving. "We'll wait until then, shall we, and surprise everyone. Was that all?"

"I think so. Oh—oh yes, and I found that funny little Mrs Kundry from next door picking herbs in my garden. She said Miss James—your cousin—always used to let her."

"Ah yes, Mrs Kundry." Crispin James frowned slightly. "She's a little—well, simple. Don't let her be a nuisance to you."

"Oh, I'm sure she won't," Annette said quickly. "She seems very timid. I gather Miss James used to be kind to her."

"My cousin Louisa had her odd charities," Crispin James remarked sourly. "As I expect you've gathered, she was extremely wealthy and extremely miserly. Has Joanna told you about her?"

"A little."

"Poor Joanna," he said, smiling. "The old lady led her to expect a handsome legacy; in the end it all went to a cats' home. No wonder Joanna feels a little bitter on the subject of money. I, on the other hand, never expected anything, having lived on remarkably poor terms with Louisa for the last twenty years of her life, so her will was no surprise to me. I believe Mrs Kundry was upset too; she was a sort of protégé of Louisa's and got treated with what, coming from that quarter, amounted to lavishness during the old thing's lifetime, but even she didn't benefit under the will; perhaps it was the disappointment that slightly unhinged her."

"Oh, I don't think she's—"

"However, you can't be interested in all this family gossip." He eyed her shrewdly. "You are tired. I noticed it as soon as you came in. There are blue smudges under your eyes. Something has slightly upset you, and if you don't want to talk about it there's no reason in the world why you should. But sit down in the cane chair for a moment and rest. In our mutual excitement over your painting—your miraculous painting—we mustn't forget that you are still a convalescent."

Annette sat, docile and content to be directed, while he began talking to her about her handling of the tricky reflections in a picture of flood and willow trees. The cane chair, old, sagging, and comfortably cushioned, had a footrest. He made her put her feet up and flung a light woolen rug over her.

"You can't do good work when you are tired; stay there for ten minutes while I stretch a canvas. I will tell you a way to relax. Look at one of your circles on the wall—choose one in particular. Keep your eyes fixed on it. Now, recall a painting that you know very well—one of your own if you like. Imagine it in your mind's eye, superimpose it over the circle, but keep the circle still in the middle of the picture. Are you doing that? Good. Keep the picture in your mind's eye with the circle in it. Now, let yourself go, relax your arms, let yourself go limp. Your eyelids are feeling heavier and heavier—heavier and heavier. Find the centre of the circle. Now move out to the circumference. Now move back to the centre. Let your head sink back. . . ."

Annette was aware of his murmuring voice for a few minutes longer, and then it gradually receded to a great distance, her head sank into the old velvet pillow, and the paintbrush which she was still holding fell from her loosened hand. She was asleep.

Crispin James covered her more carefully with the rug and then finished the job of stretching the canvas. He placed it ready on an easel and, picking up the brush that Annette had dropped, began tapping with it meditatively on the back of a chair, looking down meanwhile at her sleeping, defenceless face.

"Well, did you find any trace of your ancestors, Mr Hanaker?" the vicar inquired.

"Not yet," Noel said cheerfully, "but I haven't given up hope. I'm going to look through Parish Registers all over the county before I go back home; my mother didn't know exactly where in this part of the world her family had come from. Thank you very much for your help, anyway, sir; I've had a most interesting afternoon going through the Crowbridge parish records."

"They make a fascinating study, do they not? I must confess that I am an addict of old parish records. This town for one has a most chequered history—with its long career as a smugglers' base, and the seventeenth-century witch-burnings, the French invasion in 1377, and the civil war when the barons held it against Henry III. Henry would never have managed to capture it, either," he added peevishly, "if it hadn't been for Prince Edward."

Noel grinned. It was plain that the vicar took these historical ups and downs as personally as the more recent and less important parish affairs that occupied his professional attention.

"More tea, Mr Hanaker?" asked the vicar's wife, smiling too as she met his eye. She was a little, round, serene-faced woman, the complete antithesis of her bony, care-worn husband who looked, with his perpetually anxious expression, like an elongated saint from an El Greco painting. "You wouldn't like a puppy, would you?" Mrs Roberts went on as matter-of-factly as if she were offering Noel another piece of toast. "He's the last of Tina's litter and very well bred, but his feet are too big. It's so difficult now—we've been giving all our friends pups for years and have really just about saturated the whole neighbourhood."

"He's certainly got a lot of appeal," Noel said, as the large-footed puppy flopped and scrambled onto one of his shoes, almost tripping over its own ears. "Only thing is, how would he feel about being transplanted to New Zealand? It seems a long way to take the little feller.—Wait a minute, though, I've got a good idea—I'd very much like to offer him to a friend of mine, if she'll have him and you don't object."

"That nice Miss Sheldon?" the vicar's wife said, and laughed outright at Noel's rueful expression. "Well, I'm sorry, my dear boy, but small towns *are* small towns. I think that's a quite excellent idea. She's a delightful girl, isn't she, and I'm sure she needs more fresh air and exercise; painting all those long hours with Mr James can't be good for a convalescent, and if she had Spondee to look after it would get her out and give her something else to occupy her mind."

"Why do you call him Spondee?"

"Because of his long feet, of course. Yes, that is a splendid plan—why didn't I think of it myself? But it will come better from you."

"I don't know that it will," Noel remarked rather glumly. "She's so wrapped up in her painting now that she hardly seems to see me."

"I know, and I *cannot approve*—just when she was beginning to take an interest in parish affairs, too. I'd say a word to Crispin James—"

"Oh, no, my dear," the vicar put in mildly.

"No, as you say, it would only make matters worse. He does *not* like my husband or myself. Rather a queer man," Mrs Roberts went on distastefully. "Really I am quite sorry he has come back to live in the town—though it was sad to see his house standing empty all those years. But let us hope he will not stay long. How I wish he would move back to France, or wherever he was, for good, and sell the house to some nice, ordinary family.

"We must be broad-minded, Mary. After all, we have nothing against Mr James except that he doesn't go to church. And he does throw a glamour on the town.

"So did Black Dowsabel, and she was burned as a witch in 1887."

"You really should not make that sort of remark, you know, my dear," her husband said gently. "In the wrong company it might be misconstrued."

She was remorseful at once. "I have a spiteful tongue, Henry, I know. Forgive me. But I'm sure Mr Hanaker is the soul of discretion—aren't you? And do take Spondee along to Miss Sheldon—that nice big garden of hers will be a splendid place for him to play."

"But you'll let me give you something for him?"

"Well you don't have to, my dear boy—after all, his feet *are* enormous, he'd never find a buyer, but if you insist. . . . Everything we get for the pups goes into the church restoration fund."

Noel duly added to the fund and took his leave, carrying Spondee, who, having been pacified with a large meal, was lethargically ready to relax on anybody who would hold him, and showed no emotion at being parted from his relieved mother.

Annette stretched and opened her eyes. Crispin James smiled at her.

"Had a good nap?"

She sat up, astonished. "Heavens, did I go right off? I'm so sorry."

"Oh, don't think like that. You must have needed the rest. You'll do all the better work for it. Wait a minute while I disentangle you from the rug—good. My man's just brought us a pot of coffee, so have a cup to wake you thoroughly, and then you can start work again. Have you planned what you are going to do next?"

"I'd better finish the picture I've begun," Annette said, strolling over to examine it. "Or no—really, there's not much left to do, is there?"

"It's a mistake to linger too long on one canvas," Crispin James agreed. "The finishing touches can be deadening."

"Now I want to do a view of the marsh from your south window."

"It's ambitious—all those flat planes of green—but, all

right, go ahead and tackle it and we'll see how you do. Have you everything you need? Fine. I have to go out now, but I'll be back presently to advise you—if you want any advice!"

The door closed gently behind him. Annette cleaned her palette, selected a new range of colours, and started work. Contrary to her usual method, she laid the colour straight onto the canvas without any preliminary sketch, painting swiftly and confidently, with bold, rapid strokes. As she worked she whistled soundlessly, always a sign of inner well-being with her, keeping her attention unwaveringly on the growing picture, stepping backwards and forwards to judge the effect at different distances.

The last patch of sunlight left the floor, starlings and gulls keened and twittered outside the big window, but she painted on, absorbed and regardless. She was entirely happy.

Dusk was beginning to fall as she walked home. She was drowsy and yet alert; she had the feeling of satisfaction that comes from having achieved good work and yet, queerly, as always after her lessons, she could hardly remember what she had done, although she seemed to have been working hard and concentratedly for hours. It sometimes troubled her that she seemed to complete so few pictures—Crispin James painted five to her one—but, as he kept assuring her, she had all her life ahead.

Mrs Fairhall let her in with the pleased, conspiratorial but slightly anxious air of a parent who has at last managed to save up enough for the longed-for new bicycle and is now wondering whether it has come too late and should have been a two-stroke.

"Come into the kitchen and see what Mr Hanaker's brought you."

"Roman pottery?" said Annette with a certain lack of enthusiasm. But when she saw Spondee sprawled in his basket, her expression deepened to dismay. "A *puppy*? What in heaven's name shall I do with it? Why should Noel imagine I would want such a thing?"

"Now, Miss Annette," Mrs Fairhall scolded, "that's no

way to receive a nice present. It was a very kind thought of Mr Hanaker's. He can see, even if you can't, that you're spending altogether too much time over your paints these days, and not getting out for enough air and exercise. Taking the puppy for walks will be a very good thing for you. Mr Hanaker said he'd be round to take you out tomorrow afternoon."

"He might have consulted me first. Suppose dogs gave me hay-fever or I couldn't stand the sight of them."

"That's nonsense, Miss Annette, and well you know it. Anyway, who could help loving him as soon as they saw him, the little bless'im," she added fondly, as the puppy rolled sleepily onto his back, exposing a spherical expanse of gold-brown stomach.

"But what about his food and so on? I don't know the first thing about looking after dogs."

"I've already been out and bought him that nice basket and some puppy-biscuit," Mrs Fairhall said reprovingly, "so there's no need to worry your head. And we'll get Mr Cardew to give him his distemper injection presently and then he'll be all Sir Garnet. Now don't you start to fuss, Miss Annette, but you can take him out for his evening trot in the garden this minute—puppies can't start too soon getting regular habits. Spondee, his name is; sounds a bit heathenish I won't deny, but Mrs Roberts christened him and she's a lady who knows what's proper, so you may be sure it's all right."

"Spondee? Millstone would have been more suitable. Though I must say," Annette added reluctantly, as the puppy staggered sleepily out of its basket, "he is rather sweet. . . ."

As she took the puppy out onto the lawn it seemed to her—though it was hard to be sure—that somebody slipped away through the dusk across the lawn. She strained her eyes but could see nothing more than a vague grey shadow. Mrs Kundry again? Getting more herbs?

Maybe a watchdog wasn't such a bad idea at that.

Yawning slightly, Annette thought: perhaps the little woman is showing her fidelity to the memory of Miss

James by haunting the garden. The lack of a legacy doesn't seem to have soured her recollections of Auntie Loo. She yawned again, summoned Spondee, and returned to the house, planning a soup-and-fireside supper and early bed. These nights she slept like the dead—dreamlessly, motionless. She had put on a little weight. Dr Whitney was pleased with her.

Spondee clambered back into his basket and settled down, head on paws. Annette thought, It was well-meant of Noel, and I daresay the little thing won't be too much of a tie. Anyway I can always give him to Mrs Fairhall—she seems very taken with him—if he interferes too much with my painting-time.

What she would do with the puppy if she returned to *Eyewitness* she did not think about at all. . . .

True to his word, Noel turned up the next afternoon to take Annette and the puppy for a walk. Mild autumn sunshine was gilding the last leaves of the Virginia creepers all along the street. It was a still day, with a touch of haze.

"I've brought the car," Noel said. "I'm taking you to Poyns Castle."

"Very nice," approved Mrs Fairhall, producing a handsome leash and harness for Spondee.

"Poyns Castle—is that the one you can see from the town wall on the marsh?"

"Yes, that's it. There isn't much more than a shell left. Henry the Eighth built it to annoy the French, and Cromwell knocked it down, or so the vicar tells me. He seems to feel strongly that Cromwell should have left it alone. But it makes a nice place to clamber about; there's a central keep with mouldings of Tudor roses on it."

Annette's interest was roused. She took a sketch-block and allowed herself to be shepherded out to Noel's ramshackle car.

"I thought it was private property, though?" she said as he drove cautiously through the twisting streets and out of the town.

"So it is. It belongs to the Crowbridge Archaeological Society, who don't allow the public in, mainly because the masonry's a bit unsafe and they can't afford to keep it repaired. But they've kindly made me an honorary member on account of my dig, and lent me a key, so I can come and go when I please. I'm taking you the long way round so we can admire it from its best side."

Poyns Castle presented a grey and quite impressive bulk as they approached. Two miles to the seaward side of the town it squatted on the flat marsh, turning a blind but menacing countenance towards France. Noel bumped his long-suffering car along a rough track that took them to within three-quarters of a mile; then they reached a wide dyke that was spanned by a foot-bridge.

"Pedestrian exercise begins here," said Noel, and helped Annette out of the car.

Their way was further barred by a locked gate on the bridge. "But," Noel said, "unlocking the gate is merely a display of archaeologistmanship and quite unnecessary; anyone can lift it off its hinges and it's quite plain that numbers of people do; I believe the castle at night is a favourite resort of lovers, falling masonry notwithstanding. I doubt if many of the archaeological society members come here after dark."

"Have you met the other members?"

"Oh well, the vicar, of course, and the old boy who edits the local paper. And I believe Crispin James is another honorary member, and one or two other people who have done good deeds for the town or distinguished themselves in some not necessarily historical way. Here we are—or rather, here you must take my word for it that we are. That's the trouble about these parts. The mist comes down so quickly that it makes you feel a proper fool: arm raised to point out the view, and fizz, it's gone; there's a nice view of the town from the castle walls, too, that I wanted to show you. Damn."

"Never mind; perhaps it'll lift again as quickly as it came down," Annette said, turning up her coat-collar.

The mist which had come down so suddenly was damp

but not cold: a bright, steamy sea-mist with the sun behind it, looking as if it must lift at any moment, and yet remarkably impenetrable. Even the opposite wall of the castle was quite invisible from where they stood, just by the main gate. It was a peculiarly eerie experience to stand with the great wall looming above their backs, looking out into pearl-coloured nothingness.

A bird cried sharply only a few yards away from them, so it seemed: "Cronk, cronk, cronk!"

"Good lord, what was that? It sounded like the Great Auk," Annette said, rather startled.

"Heron, I guess. There are lots out on these marshes. Mist magnifies sounds; he probably wasn't as near as he seemed. Darn it, if I'd been expecting this I'd have brought my tape-recorder; could have picked up some beaut bird-calls. Listen."

They listened. At first Annette would have said that the silence was complete; then she began to hear the distant baa of sheep, out on the flat levels. She caught the whistle of a plover, several times repeated, and a long, rising, bubbling call which Noel said was a curlew.

"You put me to shame," Annette said. "I know hardly any bird-songs. Are you an expert?"

"Gosh, no. It was the cart before the horse, really. I got interested in making tape-recorders in my teens, and then, of course, I looked about for something to record, and hit on birds. So while Rob was wandering round drawing the wild flowers, I was immortalising the cries of New Zealand birds. I'll give you three guesses what noise a Kiwi makes."

"Too difficult," she said, laughing. The puppy whined. "I say, Spondee doesn't like it here much. Shall we go home? It's a bit claustrophobic, isn't it, when you can't see anything?"

He said crossly, "I'd have liked you to see that view; this is very inconsiderate of Providence. I wonder if the mist goes far up; sometimes it's only about ten feet high. Hang on a minute; you stay there and I'll climb up to the top of the wall. For all we know there's brilliant sunshine up there. Here, have my windcheater to sit on. You'll find a flask of coffee in the pocket; help yourself."

"How will you get up?"

"There are the remains of a stair left in the gatehouse."

"Well, do be careful."

"Oh shucks, yes. It's as easy as houses."

"Yes, but in the mist—"

Her protest fell on emptiness; he had receded, dimmed, gone. Fighting off a sudden unreasoning impulse of panic at finding herself alone, Annette sat down on the waterproof, leaning back against a massive buttress which still felt warm from the earlier sunshine. Trying to maintain a placid and matter of-fact demeanour, she poured some coffee from the flask and took Spondee on her lap, where he immediately wriggled inside her jacket.

The coffee was very hot; she could not drink it right away. She put the cup down on the short, sheep-nibbled turf, propping it against a fallen stone, and listened for sounds of Noel's progress.

"Are you all right?" she called. "Where are you?"

There was no answer for a moment. Her words seemed to sink into cotton-wool.

Then, faintly from far above her head, she heard his voice calling; she could not distinguish the words. The next moment she was startled by a thunderous crash right beside her, so loud that it fetched out echoes from all over the ruin and roused coveys of marsh-birds to screaming protest. Something struck her leg; she felt hot, wet liquid running down it, and scrambled up instinctively, dropping Spondee, who began a shrill barking.

"My God!" Noel shouted from above her head. "Annette! Annette! Are you all right?"

She looked down at her leg and realised that the liquid on it was coffee. A huge chunk of the wall had detached itself and smashed down not two feet away from her, breaking the flask and splashing her with the contents. She felt an impulse to hysterical laughter; for a moment she had thought that it was blood on her leg.

"I'm all right," she shouted. "Quite okay. Where are you?"

There was silence for a moment, then his voice came again from a slightly different position; it seemed about fifteen feet above her head.

"I'm here on a ledge that runs round inside the wall. The annoying thing is that the bit I came along has fallen off, so there's a gap, which makes it uncommonly difficult to get back."

"Can you go on?"

"Gap that way too. If I could see more than six inches below my feet I'd climb down, but it's a bit tricky not knowing what's underneath. These walls are full of holes and loose crumbly places."

"Don't I know it," said Annette, rubbing her shin where, she decided, a stone must have struck it. "Hang on a minute. There's a buttress here that ought to make a fairly safe climb. Can you locate my voice? I'll start climbing up and kind of guide you down. Right?"

"I don't like to have you do that," Noel said doubtfully.

"Would you rather I left you on the ledge and went for help?"

"Well, no—I doubt if you could make my car go."

"All right then, here I come."

It was interesting, Annette decided, to climb up into the mist—a most unusual sensation. She jammed her toes into cracks between the great blocks of crumbling stone, and hooked her fingers over lumpy projections. She was reminded of happy rock-scrambles in China with her mother. Really it was rather fun. Besides it took her mind off the quite frightening moment when the block of masonry had landed so close to her.

A foot suddenly appeared out of the mist, feeling about for a hold close by her face. It was Noel's.

Oy! Watch your step!"

She grabbed it by the ankle and guided it to a crevice.

"Many thanks," Noel said above her head. "Miss Livingstone, I presume. You go down again, exactly the same way you came up, and I'll follow."

"That was the general idea."

Annette began cautiously lowering herself, surprised to find how much more disagreeable this was than ascending. One's feet seemed far away in the mist and out of control. Ridiculous, when one knew the ground was only a dozen feet below; it would be quite possible to jump down if it weren't for the chance of turning an ankle on a broken bit of fallen stone. As it was—

Her hands abruptly jerked away from the wall, she gave a sudden startled gasp that was half a shriek—fell—scrabbled uselessly for a hold—and landed on the grass in a shower of stones and mortar.

A moment later Noel landed beside her.

"Are you all right?" he said anxiously. "What happened? Lose your hold?"

Annette was sucking a grazed hand, while with the other hand she rubbed a bruise on her knee. She looked uneasily into the mist.

"I don't quite know. I could have sworn—it felt as if someone grabbed me by the ankle. But I must have imagined it. There's no one about, is there? Hey!" she called. "Is anybody there?"

"I expect your ankle turned over," Noel suggested, "and it felt as if someone touched it. Maybe you banged it on a bit of projecting stonework."

"If you don't mind my saying so," Annette remarked somewhat acidly, "your ideas of gentle exercise and fresh air for convalescents are quite out of the common way. This little constitutional ought to set me up for days."

He looked contrite.

"I'm most terribly sorry—no, I really am. I certainly hadn't planned anything like this. Here, have a swig of coffee and we'll go straight back. I can't apologize deeply enough."

"No, you can't! And anyway there's no coffee; that little chunk of castle fell on it. Too bad about your flask."

"Good God," Noel said, horrified, going down on his knees to inspect the block of stonework. "That must weigh half a ton—no wonder it left a gap—"

"Imagine the gap it would have left if it had landed on me."

"I am thinking of that! Let's get away from here."

"We still have to find Spondee. I lost him in the excitement."

"Oh, hell. Does he answer to his name? Spondee, Spondee!"

"Pup, pup, pup, pup, pup!" called Annette.

Noel whistled, long and fruitlessly.

"Blast the little beast. I'm beginning to be sorry I gave him to you."

"Oh, but he's sweet," Annette said perversely. "I'm just getting fond of him."

She wandered away from the castle wall, whistling, calling, and straining her eyes to peer into the mist. "He can't have gone very far. His method of progression is not rapid."

"You go that way, I'll go this. Keep calling so I know where you are."

The mist swallowed Noel. Annette walked cautiously forward, feeling her way through the dimness. Romantic tales of heroines lost in fog and wandering on marshes came back to her: quaking bogs, in which people sank without a trace, or perhaps just leaving one diamond bracelet suspended from a bullrush, or a skeleton hand sticking out of a mudhole. She planted her feet firmly on the sheep-track she was following. All it needed now, she thought, was for a Hound of the Baskervilles to come baying out of the mist, eyes flaming like torches, and she would panic, lose her sense of direction, and run shrieking into the nearest quagmire. Still, really it would not be very easy to lose one's sense of direction here; though the castle had now vanished, a wan, ghostly sun, about the size of a silver threepenny bit, peered over her right shoulder; if she circumnavigated the castle, the sun would presumably slip round to her left.

"Dog, dog, dog!" she called. "Pup! Hound!"

Was that a faint whimper, or the call of a marsh-bird? She moved forward, listening hard. No, not a bird, it was definitely a whimper, coming from somewhere ahead and to her left, away from the castle.

"I believe I've found him," she called back to Noel, but no reply came; Noel must be right round on the other side of the castle already. The whimper was louder now, straight ahead, and she hurried along the track, which seemed to slope down here, though in the mist it was difficult to be certain.

"Pup, pup! Where are you, poor little feller?"

Quite close now, the whimper was, quite loud; was the puppy caught in some way, stuck in mud or tangled in brambles? I hope all this won't be a traumatic experience for him, Annette thought. I'll hardly dare confess to Mrs Roberts that the first time I took her puppy out I lost him on the marsh. But darn it, spaniels are supposed to be waterdogs, aren't they? You take them out wild-fowling and they go plunging away into the reeds and come back, mallard in mouth, with their feathery legs and tails all wet and covered in mud—

"Spondee! Puppy! Where the devil are you? I—*help!*"

The last word was wrenched out of her in a gasp as the path crumbled to void before her and, unable to stop in time, she plunged violently forward into eight feet of black, icy dyke water.

"It must have been a marsh-bird that you heard," Noel said, not for the first time. He was sitting by Annette's bed while the shocked Mrs Fairhall bustled around with beef tea and hot bottles. Dr Whitney had been and gone after reassurances that no particular harm seemed to have come to Annette's unexpected immersion—nothing, he said, that plenty of warmth and a day in bed wouldn't put right, thanks to Mr Hanaker's speedy rescue.

"Though climbing up castle walls and roaming about on marshes in dense mist is not just the sort of exercise I would prescribe to a young lady not long over pneumonia," he added severely, and Mrs Fairhall echoed his sentiments.

"Walking the puppy is one thing, Mr Noel, leading him and Miss Annette into antics like this is what I don't approve of and never shall. Lucky we are they didn't both catch their deaths!"

Poor Noel tried to mitigate his disgrace by pointing out that if Annette had not gone darting off after imaginary puppy-whimpers the accident need never have happened.

"But Noel, I could have sworn it was his voice. It was exactly like his whimper—not a bit like a snipe or whatever you said."

"Well, just the same, my dearest girl, it must have been a snipe, because by the time you'd heard it and plunged to your doom I'd already found Spondee and was on my way to look for you. Lucky I was, too; those water-weeds were the toughest things I've ever encountered. I hope I'll never come nearer to pulling my arms out of their sockets. It was like getting a mouse out of the glue tin."

"I suppose you've had frequent experience of that?" she suggested dryly. "Oh heavens, a whole day in bed; I shall be bored. There are so many things I want to get on with."

"Now, Mr Noel, Miss Annette needs her sleep, so you run along; you ought to get out of those wet clothes yourself. You can come round to see her tomorrow morning with some nice magazines or a few grapes."

"Kicked out of the nursery!" Noel said, grinning, and waved to Annette from the door. But as he ran down the stairs his expression sobered. All very well to make light of the episode, but if he had not been close at hand to free Annette from the weeds and hurtle her home at a frantic sixty miles an hour along the rutted track, things might have turned out very differently.

Moreover one thing puzzled him and made him faintly uneasy; if that had really been a woman pushing a wheelchair, that dim figure half seen, for a moment, scurrying away into the mist, why had she not paid any attention to Annette's cry, to Noel's own calls for assistance? Why had she fled off across the marsh as if the devil were after her?

Noel walked slowly along Crossbow Lane, unappreciative of the black-and-white timbered houses, the creepers, the multicoloured cobbles. A woman pushing a wheel-chair. What association did that have for him? Some recent occurrence—something that Annette had done, or that she had said. In the market, before the visit to his Roman villa. She had been worried. . . . But it was no use, he could not quite pin down the memory.

Full of vague compunction, longing to do something useful for Annette, he bought a lavish bunch of grapes and then went down to the town's only newsagent and got an armful of magazines—*Post*, *Life*, *Vogue*, *Queen*, and a copy of *Sweet Home*.

Returning, he rang the bell of Annette's house, thrust the magazines into Mrs Fairhall's arms with a muttered message, and hurried away, beginning now to feel the damp and stiffness of his soaked clothes.

That bundle ought to keep her amused for a while anyway, he thought.

"You haven't been working well for the last day or two," Crispin James said. "What is the matter? Are you still suffering from the effects of that unwise—*most* unwise—excursion with the young Australian?"

"New Zealander," Annette corrected mechanically. Her eyes were bright with fatigue; her hand shook a little as she tipped a flake of white delicately onto her canvas.

"Because if so I cannot recommend too strongly that you send him about his business; it is absolutely deplorable that he should lead you into escapades which might make you ill again and hinder your painting."

"Oh no, I'm all right," Annette said. She passed a hand wearily across her forehead, transferring a streak of white paint to her eyebrow. "No, it's not that at all."

"What's the trouble then? Tell me about it. You know I stand to you in the position of a sort of father confessor—anything is safe with me."

He left the picture he was working on and strolled over to her easel. His voice was grave and friendly; the acid note that always crept into it when he spoke of Noel had gone; he smiled at Annette.

She smiled back relievedly. "Well, I will tell you if you won't think me silly."

"My dear child! Is it likely? Sit down a moment. I don't, in general, approve of alcohol during working hours, but I think you need a glass of Madeira. Such a beautiful brown, isn't it; like marsh pools. Put your feet up and rest. Now tell me what the trouble is."

Annette sipped, leaning her head back against the sagging velvet pillow. The Madeira was sweet and heavy, pleasantly potent. There was a wonderful, luxurious sense of release about talking over her problems with Crispin James, a feeling she had not known since her father died. Since a long time before that, really; for months after he had become ill she had shouldered all the burdens.

"Do you remember," she said, "that night you took me to the barge race, the night we first met—"

"What a long time ago it seems now, does it not? I feel as if I had known you all my life."

"*Do* you? How extraordinary. That's just what—I didn't know . . . Well, anyway, perhaps you won't recall, but I mentioned a series that Rouart had done for *Eyewitness*."

"I remember very well," he said. "It was to be called the Horrors of Spring."

"That's it—how clever of you! Well, a few days ago, last week, my secretary from the office called on me—she was visiting her boy-friend's relations at Broadsea and thought she'd look in and see how I was getting on."

Crispin James frowned. "Inconsiderate," he said. "You ought to be left in peace, not reminded about that side of your life until you are ready for it. How can they expect you to get better if they keep bothering you? Really you should tell your housekeeper not to let people in."

"Oh no, Tilly's a sweet girl; I was delighted to see her."

"But she upset you."

"Well, it was something she said—she didn't mean to. But that's the extraordinary thing—after they'd gone I forgot all about it! For days! I suppose it was because it made me so furious," she pondered, rubbing her forehead perplexedly. "But it's most horribly worrying to be so absent-minded. I forgot the whole visit completely!"

"What was the upsetting thing she told you?"

"It was about Joanna. I know she's your cousin, but it did make me so angry—"

"Joanna is not always quite so sensible and infallible in her judgments as she appears to be," he said, beginning to frown. "What has she been doing?"

"She transferred that Rouart series from *Eyewitness* to *Sweet Home*. Without even mentioning it to me! And it was my pride, that series—I'd worked and sweated blood to get it, and to get it just right. It would have been the most important and attractive item in the magazine for six issues. And she just took it over! Rouart was furious, apparently, and one of my staff nearly resigned—"

"If your secretary is going to bring you agitating gossip like this I definitely think she ought to be restrained," Crispin James said angrily. "No wonder you're upset. Really it's the most stupid thing I ever heard, retailing such stuff and leaving you to brood over it."

"But I didn't brood! That's the worst part. It went clean out of my mind, until I happened to see one of Rouart's features in a copy of *Sweet Home*."

"And now you must try to put it out of your mind again."

"Oh goodness, how can I? I've written to Joanna—I'm thinking of protesting to the managing director—"

"Now, my dear Annette, you must do no such thing. No good can come of it; you will only harm and distress yourself. The thing is done—and no doubt Joanna had excellent reasons, which she did *not*, perhaps, confide to your little secretary. She may, perhaps, even have been instructed to make the exchange by some higher authority, for all you know. Why create useless trouble? Joanna is no doubt having a difficult time running both magazines—perhaps she is making mistakes, but when you go back, if you go back, these can be quickly rectified. Is it really so important, when you think about it dispassionately? Does not that world begin to seem a long way off?"

"Ye-es," she said slowly. "Until something brings it back. Do you remember the story of the Snow Queen?"

He smiled. "Vaguely—from my childhood days. But you are no Snow Queen, my dear Annette."

"No—not that. But there was an episode when Gerda was looking for Kay and she went to live with the witch, who took away her memory; all went well until Gerda saw a picture of a rose. She began hunting for roses in the witch's garden and couldn't find any, and that made her realise that the garden was nothing but a—a phantasmagoria. Sometimes I feel as if I were in that sort of state. . . ."

She looked about restlessly and her eyes fell on a small water-colour sketch, roughly mounted, leaning against the wall in a corner of the studio.

"Why, that's Poyns Castle, isn't it? I didn't know you'd ever done it—"

"I have done it many times," he said dismissingly. "That is an old sketch. Now my dear Annette, you must know, fundamentally, with the rational, sensible part of your mind that you are letting yourself become foolishly wrought up over mere trifles?"

"Are they mere trifles?"

"Of course they are!" he said vigorously. "Put them entirely out of your mind. Listen, and I will tell you something to distract you. What shall I tell you? About the link between Egyptian paintings and the art-forms on the sides of buses. —Shut your eyes. Relax. Think of the head of Nefertiti—"

Obediently she leaned back. His compelling voice, talking on, filled her mind. Gradually her hands began to relax at her sides. Her fingers uncurled. Her breathing became deep and even.

Then there was an interruption. Something whined and snuffled, scrabbling at the lobby door, which opened just enough to admit a small rotund gold-brown body. Spondee came skittering across the floor, his dusty ears waving like banners, and pawed clumsily at his mistress's ankles. He gave a small rejoicing bark. Annette's eyes opened wide.

"Good God!" Crispin James's face darkened with—was it, could it be rage? "Where did that thing come from?"

Annette shook herself completely awake and picked the puppy up remorsefully.

"He must have followed me. He's taken to doing it everywhere at home. I do apologise—I hope he hasn't done any damage. He's really very well trained; I don't think he would. Fancy his coming all that way along the street on his own. What a clever boy, then!"

Spondee wriggled agreeably and grinned an engaging spaniel grin. It had no mollifying effect on Crispin James.

"I cannot have animals in my studio," he said. Anger made his voice vibrate harshly. "Please take him home, Annette, and see that he does not do this again. It is abominably distracting—quite intolerable."

"Of course; I really am most terribly sorry. Oh dear, though, that will mean shutting him indoors—he can get out of the garden. Well, he'll just have to learn. I'll take him home and come right back."

"No," he said, "I do not think either of us is in the right mood for any more work now. I will see you again tomorrow, in the morning early."

He turned on his heel and the house door closed behind him, leaving Annette gazing after him in troubled surprise. The offence seemed a small one for such a disproportionate display of annoyance. But perhaps Crispin James was allergic to dogs.

The puppy whined hopefully and licked her chin.

VI

Three Saturdays later Noel persuaded Annette to come and see the latest progress at his Roman villa—mainly because Crispin James had been reluctantly caught up in arrangements to make a speech at the Crowbridge Michaelmas fete and so she had a free morning.

"If you don't come soon it will have to be next year—if I'm here," Noel said. "Pretty soon we shall have to pack up for the winter. Ground gets too hard. We've been lucky not to have any frosts."

Rather contrite, for she had put him off at least half a dozen times with various excuses, she let him drive her out, duly strolled round the trenches, and admired the work. A bleaching tank had been discovered, and a rather pleasant threshold mosaic of a barking dog.

"He looks a bit like Spondee," Noel said. "By the way, where is Spondee?"

Annette looked troubled and guilty.

"Mrs Fairhall's looking after him," she confessed. "The trouble is, he's got out so many times and followed me along to Crispin James's studio while I'm working there and—and Mr James doesn't like that at all. It—it makes him cross. He said he couldn't go on teaching me unless— So Mrs Fairhall said she'd look after Spondee for a week or two, till he's got out of the habit. Otherwise he just cries and cries. . . ."

"You mean you've given him to her," Noel said. He did not say it accusingly; he sighed, turning away, his hands dropping to his sides in a defeated gesture.

"Oh, Noel, I'm sorry," Annette said. "I suppose the trouble is that really I'm not a dog person. I don't know how to train them properly. I'm sure he'll be very happy with Mrs Fairhall; she adores him. She'll spoil him to death. —What are these trenches over here? The stables? Goodness, I didn't know Romans went in for riding to such an extent; I imagined them walking everywhere. Aren't they huge!"

She wandered about, admiring and making the correct remarks. Noel rather gloomily followed her. A brisk wind had whipped pink colour into her cheeks. But Noel, looking beyond the colour and superficial appearance of well-being, was troubled by a queer lassitude about her which he had not noticed when they first met.

"What have you been doing besides painting? I've hardly seen you for weeks."

"Living a hermit's life," Annette said, smiling. "About the only person I see besides Crispin James is my funny neighbour."

"Who's that?"

"Mrs Kundry. Sometimes I think Mr James is right and that she is a bit simple—she's so queer in her manner, as if she were hiding something. She haunts my garden at all hours of the day—and night—at least I suppose it's she who wanders about at night with a torch. Odd things get left behind—children's toys mostly. I've given up bothering about them; they're always removed again. I gather she had expectations from the will of my predecessor in the house, but was disappointed."

"Doesn't sound a very satisfactory neighbour," Noel said dubiously. "Why don't you see more of Mrs Roberts?"

"Oh, she fusses about my health! And I daren't confess that I've got rid of Spondee. But Mrs Kundry's harmless enough. I think she's fond of me, in her way. Tell me about your plans—shall you go back to New Zealand when the dig's finished?"

"Haven't decided yet. There isn't the right kind of history for me in New Zealand. If I went back I'd have to switch over to prehistory."

"Maori?"

"Perhaps—or earlier still. Or maybe I'll go somewhere else—Egypt, Israel. I'll go back to New Zealand first, though; I'm homesick. It's a wonderful country, you know, visually: volcanoes, hot springs, great trees—I wish I could persuade you to come and see it." There was an oddly pleading note in his voice. Usually so confident, he now seemed unsure of himself, diffident, almost humble.

"On a holiday, do you mean?"

Annette was slower-witted than usual these days; her mind seemed reluctant to focus on anything but colour and form and shape.

"Yes—if you like. Or—or—you could consider marrying me."

"*Marrying* you?" she was astonished. "But we hardly know one another!" She wasn't sure whether she was meant to take him seriously.

"But we like what we do know. Don't we? And I'd take tremendous care of you."

"Everyone takes care of me," Annette said, smiling. "Dr Whitney is full of good advice. And Mr James is always making me relax and put my feet up."

"Oh—Mr James!" Noel's goodhumoured face took on a guarded, almost sulky expression.

"It's very, very sweet of you, Noel, I'm—I'm honoured," she said, summoning her sleepy faculties together. "But it wouldn't do. I'm so sorry about it."

Exasperatedly he felt that, as on previous occasions, her attention had wandered away from him and she hardly knew what she was saying.

"Why wouldn't it do?"

"I haven't the time to spare. Oh, it sounds silly but—you do see, don't you? How busy I am? I can't really concentrate on anything but painting just now."

"Your job?" Noel said dryly. "Don't you want to get back to that?"

"Oh yes—very soon." Annette looked fleetingly disturbed. "In a month or so." She saw Noel's slightly baffled expression and put a hand on his arm. "Noel dear, you're such a sweet person—we get on so well together.

I'm sure you really understand? Can't we leave it like this?"

"Oh, yes, I understand, all right," he said with a certain grimness.

Catching sight of the time on his watch, Annette went on:

"And I'm sorry—but please will you drive me back? I promised Mr James I'd go round and work from twelve till one."

How about coming with me for a drive and tea somewhere this afternoon? We could go to Canterbury and look at the cathedral."

"I'd have loved to, but Mrs Roberts sent a note asking if I'd help with the stalls. It's a horrid nuisance; I'd much rather not. But Mr James is going to be there sketching people's portraits at ten shillings a time—it makes him very bored but of course it's the most tremendous draw. Will you be there?"

"I doubt it very much," said Noel in exasperation, and followed her to the car.

Annette stopped painting at ten to one and took a trugful of flowers along to the town hall, a noble timbered structure in the High Street, all that remained of the monasterial dining chamber. Halfway along Benedict Street she came face to face with Joanna and Philip.

"Darling!" fluted Joanna. "The very person above all others that we were hoping to see."

"Why—hullo," Annette said, astonished and rather embarrassed. "Are you down here for the day?"

"Well—for the *weekend,* actually, my dear—I meant to ring you up yesterday but Friday's always such a rush. We're putting up at the Bell so as to give the minimum of trouble all round."

We?

Annette studied the pair. All of a sudden she felt shabby and countrified in her old shirt and painting trousers. Joanna was looking smugly radiant; she had on a new limegreen suit, tremendously chic. Nobody else having Joanna's round face and pink complexion could have got away with it. But there was no denying that, worn by her, the suit had the essence of what the French call *chien.* Philip also looked excessively spic-and-span and pleased with himself; it did not need his proud proprietorial glances at Joanna's ring-finger to establish the reason.

"The fact of the matter *is*, darling—and as you're such an old friend I'm delighted that you're one of the *first* to hear—Philip and I are engaged, and we've come down here to have a little teeny quiet weekend to ourselves out of all the hurly-burly and nods and becks and wreathed smiles at the office. Well, you know how they are."

"Congratulations to you both," Annette said formally. Evidently it was tacitly proposed that they should all agree to forget Philip's earlier engagement. Ignoring an inner quirk of sardonic amusement, she fell in with this arrangement. She was surprised to find how little the news affected her; scrutinising Philip now, dispassionately, she wondered how she could ever have been bowled over by his facile, self-satisfied charm.

And how could Joanna . . . ? But as she smiled at Joanna and made the correct inquiries about wedding dates, and watched her dear friend sparkling, cooing, and preening like a plump, self-satisfied turtle-dove with a hint of malice in its eye, Annette found herself suddenly boiling with a healthy and honest rage. It was so obvious that Joanna had dragged Philip down here in order to show him off, to needle Annette just a little bit further. She was making an all-out effort to get Annette's job away from her; did she have to do this as well? And the fact that Annette had, by chance circumstances, been armoured against such a blow was no mitigation of her behaviour.

"And will you stop working when you marry?" Annette could not resist asking.

"Darling, *hardly!* I can't quite see myself in checked gingham yearning over the kitchen sink. Or no, it's cradles one yearns over, isn't it? . . . But now, love, dump that opulent Lady Bountiful freight of flowers and come along to lunch at the Bell—if Phil isn't allowed to order some champers soon he'll feel he's been lured down here under false pretences."

"Well—I'm not sure—" Annette said.

"Oh, now, *darling!* If you hum and haver and demur I shall think I don't know what! Besides, Cris will be there, and he'll be terribly bored if you don't come—he talks of nothing but you, I assure you!"

"I'll have to change then—"

"Why, *no*, sweetie—come as you are; you're perfectly genteel, I assure you—*quite* good enough for all those old trouts at the Bell."

Annette stood firm on this point, however; depositing her flowers at the hall, she darted home and changed into a lavender-coloured wool dress with a wide black belt. It had been one of her favourites but was still much too loose on her: damn. Too late to change again, though.

She was unfeignedly glad of Crispin James's presence through the slightly forced gaieties of the betrothal lunch; several times, looking up to find his brilliant dark eyes fixed on her, she felt as if he were extending a steadying hand to guide her through a treacherous quicksand.

Sipping her champagne, she suddenly thought of Noel Hanaker and glanced round the dining-room in search of him. But he was not to be seen, and she concluded that he had gone back to the villa to make the most of the daylight. Up to this moment she had forgotten about his unexpected proposal of marriage; now it came back into her mind. Had he really meant it? He had not said he loved her, or made any declaration of that kind. It was more as if he wanted to rescue her from something—but from what? Too much safety, placidity, solitude, convalescence, in Crowbridge?

Amused at the idea, she let her eyes wander round the oak-beamed dining-room, over the hearty red faces, the tweeds and pearls of the other lunchers, talking in their confident country voices and disposing of pheasant stuffed with prunes or Irish stew and dumplings according to taste. Perhaps it was from dullness and mediocrity that

Noel wanted to rescue her? But then her eyes found those of Crispin James and she felt that she was in no danger of dullness. She forgot once more about Noel, who, out at the site, in a biting wind and under a sky that promised rain, was munching ham sandwiches and planning drastic action.

Town fetes are very similar one to another and that at Crowbridge ran according to pattern, with fancy-work, jumble, crowds of pushing, elderly women intent on bargains, side-shows, amateur theatricals, children dropping lollies on the floor, and, since rain had moved the operation indoors, a strong and pervasive smell of paraffin and damp clothes.

Crispin James, sitting on a dais and sketching portraits for ten shillings apiece, seemed as out of place as a Lippizaner on a milk-round. Annette, remembering that he had said he hated doing portraits, watched him from the antique stall, where she was helping, with amazement and admiration. How well he was doing it—talking to the sitters and drawing them out, joking, making them feel interesting and important so that instead of sitting like stuffed dummies, paralysed with shyness, they laughed and talked and revealed themselves to him.

Joanna and Philip paid a duty-call to the festivities with self-conscious smiles on their faces, and Annette saw Joanna displaying her ring to various old ladies, presumably acquaintances of her Auntie Loo. They worked their way round to Annette, and Philip—with an odiously patronising manner, Annette said to herself—bought a miniature basket made of shells for sixpence and presented it with a flourish to Joanna.

"Is that all I get for an engagement present, you wretch?" she said, twinkling up at him. "Annette, love, I'd never have *imagined* you'd grace a bazaar stall so well. As to the manner *born,* my dear! Phil, I think we've done our duty now, don't you, mopping and mowing to all the old things; how about getting the car out and running over to Dungeness?"

"Come to my house for a meal this evening," Annette suggested.

"Darling, we'd have *adored* to, but we're booked to go over to some friends at Broadsea. But perhaps tomorrow? *Perfect*. Now *don't* stay too long and kill yourself with fatigue, my love. Come on, Phil." She tucked her hand through his arm and they sauntered out looking gay and free; Annette glanced after them rather enviously.

When her relief took over she strolled round the stalls, buying, as in honour bound, a great many things she neither wished for nor needed. All of a sudden she felt frighteningly bored and longed for London, the commitments of her job, and some intelligent conversation.

Almost involuntarily she made her way towards Crispin James, who had just finished a portrait and was signing it before handing it with tremendous gallantry to the delighted subject, a lady in her middle sixties with such a pronounced resemblance to a turkey that it was quite a surprise to hear her talking English.

"I shall treasure it, Mr James, treasure it," she gobbled, tucking the sketch carefully into a large plastic bag before moving off into the crowd. Annette continued to edge her way towards the dais, and was witness to an odd little incident.

The throng was so thick in the hall that anyone more than a couple of feet away was completely concealed. Now the mass of humanity, shifting and breaking, suddenly threw up before Crispin James's platform a small grey-haired woman pushing a wheel-chair.

There were no other candidates for portraiture at the moment, apparently, and the woman said something quietly to Crispin James, apparently a request that he should draw the person in the chair. Annette could not see who this was from where she stood, but she recognised the little woman as Mrs Kundry. Something about the chair gave her a queer jolt—where could she have seen it before?

Trying to win through to a point from which she could see the wheel-chair's occupant, she passed behind a tall man and missed the first impact of Crispin James's reaction. Stepping closer, she was thunderstruck to hear him say, in a low but carrying voice:

"Get that thing out of my sight! How dare you bring it here! Don't ever do that again!"

The savagery of his tone was a revelation to Annette. She caught a glimpse of his face, a white mask of rage, and then two stout women with baskets, pushing in front of her, screened him from view. Annette was quite glad of their intervention; the sight of his expression had been like a close view of naked lightning. Feeling curiously sick and shocked, she turned instinctively towards the entrance.

Ahead of her she saw Mrs Kundry, edging a way dexterously through the crowd with her wheel-chair. Was it a child she was pushing? Annette thought of the toys left in her garden, the torn-up plants, which she had never had the temerity to mention. Perhaps the explanation of these oddities lay here. She moved on in pursuit.

"Dear Miss Sheldon, you're not going yet? Before the children's play?" one of the organisers wailed, and she called in reply, "I'll just drop all these things I've bought at home and then come back. . . ."

It was a huge relief to get out of the door, into the fresh, rainy air. She saw Mrs Kundry some way ahead, just about to turn the corner of the street, but by taking a short cut up a flight of steps and through an alley, Annette was able to overtake and come out ahead of her.

The sight of the chair's occupant stopped her dead.

So this was the face that Crispin James had refused to draw! Could one blame him? And how odd of Mrs Kundry to want the drawing made!

For Annette herself, though, there was a queer fascination in the figure; she remembered the drawn, wild face of Mad Maggie in Brueghel's fantastic picture, and she longed to hurry home and try to get this girl's face down on paper.

But first she must ask about the toys. She stood and waited until Mrs Kundry came up with her. The little woman gave a queer, frightened gasp at sight of Annette—she had been hurrying through the drizzle with her head down and saw her only when it was too late to avoid a meeting.

"Oh, Miss—Miss Sheldon. I didn't see you—I must get home—it's late—"

She tried to edge past, but Annette turned and walked beside her. The figure in the chair was motionless, keeping its slanted downward gaze on the wet cobblestones as they slipped by.

"I'm going this way too," Annette said easily. "I just wondered—I've got a humming-top and a doll that I found in my garden—I wanted to ask if they belonged to you?"

"Oh dear," Mrs Kundry muttered, "I *thought* she'd been getting out again. But she's so artful—slips out like a ferret. I wondered about those leaves on the kitchen floor. Doris, you bad girl, you! You've been going in the garden without Mother!"

The figure in the chair gave a hoarse, inarticulate murmur but took no further notice.

"She's quiet now," Mrs Kundry confided. "I gave her a couple of tranquillisers before I came out. Well, it's hard if I can't get out sometimes to where there's people, isn't it? I like a bit of life. But I don't like to leave her in anybody else's charge. Just in case—well, you know. But I'm really sorry she's been in your garden. I'll have to keep more of an eye on her. The trouble is, she used to sleep in the attic where I could bolt her in, but since the window blew out I don't like to put her up there, and she's so clever with locks—she hides away the keys, and then when my eye's off her, when I'm watching the TV in the evenings, she can slip out in a minute."

"Can't you get the window mended?" suggested Annette. Mrs Kundry looked vague and harassed.

"They're all so slow—and they charge so, the robbers. . . . Still, she's a good girl mostly, aren't you, Doris?"

Doris made no reply.

"Wouldn't it be easier for you," Annette said hesitantly, "if she were put in—"

Mrs Kundry's face crumpled. Her voice was both angry and tearful. "Don't say it, don't! I couldn't *bear* it if she were in one of those places. She's all I've got. And one day she's going to get better and help me, aren't you, Doris? She's quite clear at times, speaks quite plain, and she understands everything I tell her. Don't you, Doris? You know when Mother wants you to do something, don't you?"

There was something almost frightening about the strength and possessiveness of the love in Mrs Kundry's voice and her eyes blazed with—what was it?—pride? "They shan't take you away from me, shall they, Doris? They shan't lock you up in one of those wicked places. You'd die, and I would too. They can't do anything as long as you're a good girl and nobody complains; they've got no right to. I'd soon have the law on them. Miss James told me that. So don't you go suggesting a cruel thing like that again, Miss Sheldon."

Annette, rather shaken by the look Mrs Kundry gave her, in which enmity and placation were uncomfortably mingled, hurried to make what amends she could.

"I'm sorry. Of course I didn't mean—It was just about the garden."

"I'm sorry about the garden, Miss Sheldon. I'll see she doesn't get in again."

"It's just that I'm a bit scared of her," Annette confessed, thinking with an internal shudder of that scarecrow, wild-eyed figure wandering loose in the dark at night. Supposing Annette had gone down that time when she saw the torch? What would have happened? And why did she keep feeling she had seen Doris before?

"She won't hurt you," Mrs Kundry assured her. "I'll take care of that. Doris, you're not to hurt Miss Sheldon. Do you understand? This is Miss Sheldon here. See her?"

Doris grunted, and surprised Annette by turning her head slowly and fixing her with those angry, dark, unfocused eyes. The exchange of looks gave Annette a queer pang—below the hostility in the cretin's gaze she sensed hurt and bewilderment like that of an ill-treated animal . . . and there was something strangely familiar about her face.

"She'll remember you now," Mrs Kundry said. "And you won't make trouble for us, will you, Miss Sheldon? I was obliged to you that other time—that was just an accident. If there got to be gossip about her in the town—stories that she could get rough—people are so spiteful . . . But they can't complain, they really can't. I keep her out of everybody's way, only go out when it's dark or bad weather. She's really harmless. But if you was to make trouble for us I—I don't know what I'd do."

What other time? Annette wondered. But now they had reached her house and she ran in and fetched the top and doll.

"There, Doris, see, the kind lady's given your things back. We wondered where they'd got to, didn't we? Say thank you."

But without speaking Doris darted out a long bony hand and snatched the things. She ducked her head, murmuring over them unintelligibly, and Mrs Kundry said a hasty goodbye and scuttled on to her own house.

Annette went pondering indoors. Why had Crispin James been so angry? How well did he know Mrs Kundry? And what had Mrs Kundry meant by "that other time"?

She felt even less inclined to return to the heat and fuss and female clamour of the fete. She dumped her purchases in the hall, made herself a cup of tea, and took it up to the studio, where she began quickly sketching down impressions from memory of Doris, the drawn face, half-open mouth, gaunt ungainly figure, and those dark inimical eyes with spite behind their wondering stare.

As usual when Annette drew, time fled past and she was startled by the muffled boom of the church clock striking six, which came faintly to her, blown on the rainy wind. Heavens! And she had promised to go back and see the children's play. Well it was too late now. She stretched her cramped wrist, shuffled the drawings together, and put them in a portfolio. The cup of tea had long since grown cold and scummy; she had forgotten it. Transported away from real life by the act of drawing, she had been in a dream, the dream that consciously or subconsciously now occupied most of her waking hours. So soon as her mind was released from immediate practical demands a gravitational pull swung it back into the orbit of Crispin James.

Her thoughts played round him incessantly, obsessively; now it was some remark of his that she slowly probed for its full meaning; now some detail from one of his pictures occupied her attention; now a memory of his physical presence grew in her mind like a great dark tree until it had withdrawn the life from everything else.

She was pondering over something he had said about drawing hands, and her memory had drifted back to one of his drawings of hands, and to his own hands themselves: strong, spatulate, long-fingered. She stood absently staring at her own fingers while the undercurrent of her mind still played over his curious behaviour with Mrs Kundry and Doris—why had he been so angry?

She could give herself no answer to this why? but was still circling aimlessly round it when the doorbell rang and the caller, discovering that the front door was on the latch, pushed it open and walked into the hall.

"I'm up here," Annette called. She heard steps on the stairs, and Crispin James himself appeared in the doorway. His hair was ruffled by wind and slightly damp; his eyes had that inward look which comes from walking in the dark and rain.

"I had to come and see you," he said quickly without preamble. "The fete's only just finished. God, these festivities! Never again. I've been thinking about you for the last two hours."

Annette looked at him wonderingly. She said nothing. She lived so much with the idea of him nowadays that his actual presence hardly seemed more tangible than a dream.

He came forward into the room.

"I haven't been up here before," he said. "It's a good room."

She had hung the walls, above the panelling, with natural-coloured hessian, and scraped the floor to a golden plainness. An easel, a few chairs, and a big table were the only furniture in the room. Heating came from concealed electric panels. There were no curtains. Rain silvered the one wall-sized window which held away the blackness of the garden outside.

Crispin James walked across the room, inspected a sketch on the easel, and turned on his heel. He stared frowningly at Annette as if choosing the order of his words. A large flat dish of green apples stood on the table; he picked one up and held it like a demonstration specimen.

"If you're a painter," he said abruptly, "you have to fight. You have to fight all the time against ugliness and stupidity and ignorance. You see that, don't you?"

"Yes," said Annette. She had a feeling of suffocation. Something had happened to her breathing—it came in uneven jerks, counterpoint to the thumping of her heart.

He crossed to where she stood and looked down at her. "You were there this afternoon, weren't you? Yes, I know you were. I saw your white face in the crowd. When you are tired or unhappy your skin goes transparent white, like a wood-anemone—I wanted to take you away and give you peach brandy, wrap you up in fur. . . . But you vanished before I could disentangle myself from all those worn-out old bodies, those old culls." His voice sharpened with contempt.

"I was afraid—" Annette began. "I thought you were angry—"

"I was, blazing angry—but not with you, my pretty. Never in my life with you. It was that pair—that fool of a woman, that obscene girl. I would never—God in heaven, *what's that?"* His eyes, dilating, fixed on something that lay behind Annette. Turning, she saw that it was a stray sketch, one of the portraits of Doris that must have fallen and been overlooked when she put the others away.

"Where did that come from?" The apple he had been holding fell to the floor. He was grasping Annette's hand so tightly that she felt her bones grind together. He jerked her violently round to face him and she saw that his eyes were narrow with rage.

"Did you do that sketch?"

"Yes," she stammered. "Don't! You're hurting me!"

"From the model?"

"No, from memory. Why?"

"Why? Why did you do it?"

"Why not? Her face interested me, that's all. Oh, please let go!"

He loosed her hand, stooped, and with a quick gesture, as if even the touch of the paper repelled him, tore the sketch across and across, throwing the scraps onto the floor.

"Don't ever do that again! Never! Understand?"

"But why not? What's wrong with it?" said Annette rather piteously.

"It's like drawing filth! That face is straight from hell. From the dark, evil side of things. I forbid you even to think about it. How could you do it? You don't hang over cesspools, or stare at offal in butchers' windows—you should be sweet, and clear, and calm, not—"

He stopped short. Annette was looking at him dazedly, her great dark eyes fixed with wonder on his face as if she were powerless to prevent his dealing her blow after blow.

"Forget all about her!" he said savagely. "Forget her, forget her!"

And he took Annette roughly in his arms, turning her face up to his, and kissed her hard and mercilessly, bearing her down, as if he were trying to blot out the image of that other face. The room, the house, the whole planet whirled in a giddy orbit beyond her closed eyes; she leaned against him almost fainting and felt the strength and anger of his body as the one certainty in a cloud of bewilderment.

When at last he released her neither of them spoke. Crispin James took her hand and led her from the studio and downstairs and she followed docilely to the sitting-room, where he set her in a chair by the fire, found a glass, and splashed brandy into it.

"Drink that," he said in a harsh voice. She drank obediently, feeling, as if from a distance, the heat of the spirit race through her. She sat staring down at the oily rings left by the brandy on the clear, bluish glass, turning the glass in her fingers, while every particle of her being, blood and breathing and memory and perception, swung and steadied into a new course. If asked, she could not have said whether she was happy or in anguish, but she felt a queer tranquility, as if this were a moment she had been waiting for all her life.

Crispin James, leaning on the mantelpiece, looked down at her. His gaze travelled round and through her, searchingly, as if he would have liked to absorb the whole essence of her into himself.

"I want to marry you. When? Next week?"

Was he really speaking?

"I don't know," said Annette. "I suppose—as soon as you like. When you like," she said again dreamily after a pause, looking into the barred and glowing recesses of the fire.

"As soon as I can arrange it, then. We'll get away from here. Travel; go abroad somewhere, find some sun. I'll teach you how to paint palm trees. And flamingoes."

A vision drifted across the fire for Annette of desert, camels, pyramids, herself and Crispin James, incredibly together forever, watching the tattered magnificence of some Arabian sunset. She could not smile or speak, but a deep sigh stirred her, like wind on sand.

"I'll leave you now," Crispin James said. "You're tired; you must rest. You should have a hot drink and go to bed. Will you do that?"

"Yes."

"Do you promise?"

"Of course."

She rose automatically to say goodbye. He put his arms round her again, and his lips drove against hers for a long, uncharted time, until the whole of her consciousness seemed to evaporate and be lost in his.

When the front door slammed behind him and his footsteps died away along the street she still stood by the fireplace, gazing into the red depths of the fire, rubbing her bruised wrist with heedless fingers. Presently, recollecting herself a little, she went to the kitchen and heated up some milk. While she was drinking it the telephone began to ring, a tremulous insistent needle of sound in the silent house. But she sat by the fire, sipping the hot milk, and took no notice. After a time the ringing stopped.

Annette woke up next day to a mood of sheer terror. It was a Sunday, cold, grey, and rainy; except for church-bells ringing to eight o'clock matins, the town was wrapped in weekend hush: no voice, footstep, car, or cycle bell broke the silence in which she lay wrestling with her causeless fright. She should have been ecstatically happy, and part of her was; at the remembrance of Crispin James's kisses her body began to tremble and she felt actually faint with longing for their repetition. But far back in her mind some panicky rear-guard from her sane, cautious, career-self kept crying, "Watch out, don't let yourself be submerged! It's dangerous to plunge so deeply! Keep something back, keep a little nucleus of your own."

Oh, she thought, tossing and turning restlessly, if only I could get away for a little to my job, if I had that to fall back on!

Unable to lie still any longer, she swiftly bathed and dressed, ate some fruit, and took the car down along the marsh road to Ayling Strand, where a wind-swept line of sand dunes marked the division between marsh and sea. She left the car on the landward side of the dunes and ploughed across their shifting, slippery slopes till she came to the beach itself: a flat, wide, shining expanse of sand with the sea a far-distant thread on the horizon. Not another soul could be seen, which was hardly surprising on a bleak and drizzling November morning. Annette started walking at a good pace along the shore, keeping a casual eye open for shells and odd pieces of driftwood to add to a collection of *objets trouvés* that she was making.

I am being foolish, she told herself resolutely. If I am not the luckiest person in the world, there can be few luckier; to have my own house, more money than I can spend, my painting, and then to be loved by, to be in love with, such a genius as Crispin James—what more can I possibly want?

I want to meet him on equal terms, her rear-guard self suggested. And that he will never allow.

She imagined herself trying to stand up against him, and the inevitable overthrow; at the thought such a weakening, overwhelming rush of tenderness engulfed her that she almost cried out; she turned and pushed back in the face of the rainy wind, walking frantically fast as if she were trying to outpace her own anxieties.

"Hey!" yelled a voice to her right, "are you doing this for a bet, or may I come and join you?"

She turned to see Noel come scrambling over the dunes towards her.

"I saw your car parked by the road," he panted. "Just off for my Sunday morning dig, but the weather was so nasty I was in two minds about packing it in. Doesn't deter you, though, I see; healthy is as healthy does. Hats off to the island race."

"New Zealand is an island too, I understand," Annette said primly.

"Several. But we don't make quite such a thing about it. Do you know, you look about fifteen in those trousers and that parka affair. Suits you." He fell into step beside her. "How did the fete go? Did you sell many whateveritwases?"

"I left before the end; I went home and did some drawing." Remembering the sequel to her drawing, she fell silent. There was a pause.

"Listen—about your painting," Noel began presently,

"I know it's no business of mine and you're quite at liberty to tell me to go and fry my face but—oh hell—"

She turned to him interrogatively, and the sight of her candid eyes seemed to give him courage.

"Crispin James, now—I've been wondering if I ought to warn you that he's rather a queer personality. Rob, my brother in Paris—"

"Look," Annette said quickly—it was almost a reflex—"before you say anything I must tell you that Crispin James and I are going to be married."

"*What?*"

Automatically they had halted and turned to face one another; Annette thought fleetingly how absurd they must look, standing like puppets in the middle of the wide, empty beach.

It seemed to take a moment for Noel to register the full import of her news; then he said:

"Oh. Oh I see. Yes, of course, that makes a difference."

He stood without speaking for a moment or two more, tracing aimless patterns in the sand with a stick he had picked up. Then he summoned resolution and went on hesitantly, "I'm sorry, Annette. Lord knows you can say I hardly know you and I've no call to interfere, but I think you're doing a wrong thing—wrong for you, I mean. Why, apart from everything else, he's nearly twice your age."

"You're perfectly right," Annette said coldly, "and I really can't see that it's the slightest business of yours."

"Hell," Noel went on, frowning, half to himself, without taking much notice of what she had said, "that really is the devil of a complication."

"What did you mean by 'apart from everything else'?" Annette couldn't help asking curiously.

"The painting, of course."

"Painting?" She was bewildered. "I thought perhaps you meant he was after my money."

"Money? Have you any money? I didn't know."

"But what has painting to do with it?"

"My dear girl," he said furiously, "it has *everything* to do with it. There's something fatal about him—can't you feel it? Tell me truly, are you happy about your painting, about what he's teaching you? If you are, if you really are, I'll shut up and go away."

"Of course I am."

"Honestly?"

"Do you think I'd lie about it?" said Annette angrily, and was thunderstruck to find that she was crying; tears were streaming in a cascade down her face and she seemed absolutely powerless to stop them.

"Oh lord, I'm an oaf," Noel said desperately. "Here, use mine, use my shirt if you want. I do nothing but make a mess of things. Please can you forget the whole affair?" He mopped her face with awkward friendliness. "I've said much more than I should. Can you try to forgive me?"

After a while she nodded, blowing her nose, and his strained face lightened a little.

"But look—do pay attention now," he said earnestly. "Will you remember this: if ever you want to know anything that—that you think I might be able to tell you—or if you need any help—will you let me know?"

"All right," said Annette. "If it will make you feel better. But really I don't know what you're talking about."

"Never mind," said Noel. "Only remember that I do most truly want to help you. —I think I'd better be off now before I make an even bigger fool of myself. Goodbye."

He bent and swiftly but gently kissed her cheek; next minute he was walking out across the sand towards the sea, his tall, thin figure expressing a sort of lonely resolution.

VII

Annette turned and made her way over the dunes to her car, ducking her face against the cold persistent rain. The long, grey day stretched ahead of her.

By noon she had run out of cigarettes. The shops were all Sabbath-shut so she walked along to the Bell, devoutly hoping that none of the three visitors with whom she was acquainted would be there. Noel, she was fairly sure, would be out at his dig, and it seemed likely that Joanna and Philip would be lunching elsewhere with friends. She felt, still, mentally stiff and shocked from her encounters with Noel and with Crispin James and could hardly face the prospect of talking to anybody else; the world of painting where she mostly lived at present was too remote for rapid social adjustment. She had an odd, undefined sensation that her face and body were away out of reach, hardly under control of her mind, and the last thing she wanted was to be called on to make any conversational effort, at least before several more hours had passed.

She was out of luck, however.

As she crossed the Turkey-carpeted, antlered lobby to the little grille where cigarettes could be bought, a voice called to her through a doorway.

"Yoo-hoo, dearie! Come and keep me company."

She turned and saw Joanna, animated and sparkling in dark blue with white ruffles, perched on a stool in the lounge bar.

Joanna beckoned imperiously and Annette reluctantly joined her.

"Darling, what a bit of luck! Only think, Phil's gone off to play *golf*, of all things, in the wet, and here I am, lone and lorn. What a prospect for our married life! Now, tell me, what will you *drink? Tomato* juice? My angel! What's come over you?"

Annette said, untruthfully, that she had a headache, and, to turn the conversation from herself, asked questions about Joanna's and Philip's plans after they were married. Thus diverted, Joanna spun easily enough into a discussion of flats and furnishings, gadgets and schemes of decoration.

"And what would you like for a wedding present?" Annette presently asked.

"Oh, my honey! It seems such a *sordid* subject! Still, it would be folly to be coy, wouldn't it? When you're so nicely fixed. Well, to be candid, we'd adore a *dishwasher*. We've got most other things—of course *Sweet Home* are doing us proud with premium offers and wholesale prices. By the *way,* sweetie, regarding your *letter,* I didn't like to raise the matter in general conversation, but of course I quite *understand. Naturally* you were upset about the Rouart series, but you can guess how it was: the Man. Dir. practically held a *gun* at my head, so my hands were *tied*. What could I do? You do see, don't you?"

"Oh yes, I see," Annette said wearily. Another time, she told herself, she would join battle over this issue; today she really could not.

"Ducky, how *are* you?" Joanna said, regarding her shrewdly. "You look ravishing of course—you should always wear grey—but just the least bit *tired*. Is old Cris working you too hard? And haven't you lost weight? You put me to shame, with my frenetic, *broken reed* attempts to diet, you just look like a reed *naturally*. It is unfair!"

Annette said thank you, and she was quite well really.

"Enjoying the painting? Meeting some pleasant souls down here? I noticed that bearded digger at breakfast—what's his name, Hemstitch, Hamster? I'm sorry to see *he's* still around."

"Oh yes," Annette said vaguely. The mention of painting had taken her mind back to the studio. "Yes, he's still here. He asked me to marry him yesterday."

"Marry you?" Joanna looked thunderstruck. "*That* man? Good gracious, my dear, what absolute impertinence! Blatant *fortune* hunting. I hope you turned him down flat."

"Oh, but he's very nice; I like him. Look, there are Philip and a man—I must really go home, I've lots to do. But you're coming round this evening, aren't you? See you then. As early as you like."

Annette managed to slip away with no more than a wave and a smile while Philip and his golfing partner were still saying goodbyes. She did not look back, and thus missed the angry, calculating look that Joanna shot after her.

The rest of the day dragged, and was queerly tiring; in spite of her excuse to Joanna, Annette found it hard to settle to any occupation. The drizzle made work in the garden unattractive, and she had no picture started in her own studio that she wanted to continue. Various scruples prevented her going round to Crispin James's, and though she thought of him constantly and hoped he would call, he did not do so. Why not? she wondered.

By five she was longing for a bath and bed, and awaited the arrival of Joanna and Philip without enthusiasm. Such self-command as remained to her was beginning to slip; she wondered if she would have the energy to countenance the billing and cooing of the engaged couple. She hoped they would leave early for their drive back to London. Dr Whitney, whom she had invited to make a fourth, rang up to say that he had been called out on a maternity case and doubted if he could get back.

Doggedly Annette resolved that her entertainment should be as impeccable as possible, and she made a clam chowder, from a recipe bequeathed to her by her mother, concocted a sweet from blueberries and whipped cream layered between slivers of flaky pastry, and made sure that her silver and glassware was polished to the last degree of frosty perfection. She was glad that it was Mrs Fairhall's evening off and that she had the preparation of the meal to occupy her; the work removed the need for thought. And her thoughts were disjointed and unhappy, to be avoided if possible.

At ten to six, when all was ready, feeling badly in need of more steadying occupation, she went upstairs and began tidying her studio. Presently she came, with something like consternation, to the portfolio into which she had put all but one of the heads of Doris. She spread them out and considered them critically.

They were good, some of them very good. The expression was brilliantly caught.

But they were taboo.

Hesitantly she sorted through them, remembering the absolute disgust with which Crispin James had torn the other one across and across. Should she destroy them? It seemed a kind of disloyalty to him not to, but something in her rebelled at this, and suddenly she swept them all up, and, without troubling to put on a coat, ran downstairs and out of the front door to the next house. Perhaps as Mrs Kundry had been foiled in her wish to get a sketch of Doris from Crispin James's pencil, perhaps she would like to have them?

Annette rang the bell.

The usual long pause ensued, and she was almost on the point of giving up and going home again when at last she heard footsteps coming along the passage inside.

The rainy afternoon had developed into a thoroughly nasty evening—not the sort, Noel thought, on which anybody would be out, unless he were invited to a party—he happened to know this was the case with Crispin James—or were obliged to for professional reasons, such as burglary.

He gave a last careful look around Crispin James's studio, switched off his torch, and prepared to depart the way he had come, by the vestibule and the outside stairs. But at the outer door he paused, listening, with his gloved hand on the latch, and then, with great silence and expedition, slipped into the shelter of a large closet which occupied one wall of the little entrance hall and held a miscellaneous collection of painting equipment.

Two people came in from outside, shaking off the wet.

"Well," Crispin James said ungraciously, "What's this important thing you've dragged me away from the Ansons' to tell me? I suppose you'll expect to be given a drink? Whisky?"

"Darling Cris, you know you hate parties; you were only too glad to be dragged. All those old pussies! Yes, I'd like a drink, and a large one, please."

The voices passed through to the studio. The door, carelessly pulled to behind them by Joanna, did not latch. Noel came out of cover with caution, hesitated, and finally decided in favour of eavesdropping.

"My, you have been working hard, haven't you?" floated back through the opening in Joanna's silvery tones, full of false enthusiasm. "Gorgeous! *Wunderbar!* Are those yours or our little guinea pig's?"

"That's none of your business," Crispin James said angrily. "Come on—what was it you wanted to say?"

"*Dear* Cris! Not very amiable this evening? Well, firstly, I wanted to inquire if your plans—our plans—are going on as swimmingly as I hope? You seem to have worked your way well into little Annette's affections so far as one can *see*—but you have a rival. Did you know that young diggerboy from the back of beyond had proposed to her? *He* knows when he's on to a likely thing, even if you don't!"

"What? You mean Hanaker?" Crispin James sounded surprised, but not particularly dismayed. "He proposed to her? When?"

"How should I know? Bless her, her head is quite in the clouds these days. She only told me because she wanted to *annoy me*. —But you don't seem worried?"

"I'm not. He hasn't the slightest chance.

"Why? Forgive me if I seem to *press* on a personal point, but have you actually popped the question?"

"Oh for goodness' sake, Joanna, give me time—how long have I known the girl?"

"Long enough, I should have thought; anyone can see she's head over ears. Your famous charm! So how is it?"

"Well, yes, it's fixed," he said rather reluctantly. "But in any case, what does it matter to you? The main thing is that she's here, she's happy, she shows no signs of wanting to get back to the office; she's not impeding *your* activities, so far as I can make out. Only for God's sake will you be a bit more discreet in what you do at *Eyewitness*; try not to let your rapacity overcome your good sense. She was thoroughly upset at that business over the Rouart series; it took me endless trouble to get her tranquil again."

"But you did it? Philanthropist!" mocked Joanna. Then she said, softly but with venom, "You know, I really *loathe* that girl. Why should she have everything in the world: moderate ability in the office; good looks enough to be able to put it across without any effort; that diffident, appealing manner that *always* goes down well, particularly with males; the job I'm after—which they'll keep for her as long as she shows any signs of intending to come back; a quite undeserved talent for painting—and to crown it, she has to win all that money. That really put the lid on it. It's enough to make you *spit*."

"That cooked her goose, that windfall, didn't it?" said Crispin James maliciously. "I can't help feeling that her ability in the office must be rather more than you give her credit for. But will you please come to the point?"

"I've been thinking over our arrangement," Joanna explained, "and it strikes me that it's highly one-sided. It's fine for you—you get an exceedingly wealthy wife and another—well, shall we say, disciple? Jam for you all the way. But what do I get out of it all?"

"You get this coveted job, my dear Joanna—and you seem to have annexed her young man as well. What more do you want?"

"I want some of the cash," Joanna said frankly. "Getting married decently is an expensive business—Phil hasn't a sou, drachma, or rouble of his own, and I haven't absolutely got my paws on the job—*yet*. There's many a slip. I want a loan, or better still, an allowance."

"My dear girl! I haven't got the cash—*yet*."

"You must have something of your own—you give the impression of affluence."

"Overdraft," Crispin James said succinctly. "Until my next show I'm living on promises."

"I can see why you're keeping Sunshine's nose to the grindstone." Joanna's tone was thoughtfully admiring. "You really have got it all organised, haven't you, cher maitre?"

"In any case," Crispin James went on coldly, "I really fail to see why you should have these expectations. *I'm* doing all the work."

"Who took the trouble to look you up in Paris and tell you about this—shall we say, opening? Who brought her down here?"

"I could perfectly well have made her acquaintance in a dozen different ways; I had it all planned years ago when I saw one of her pictures."

"Rubbish; you'd never have bothered if I hadn't got in touch with you."

"Look, my dear Joanna, you might as well put this idea out of your head once and for all."

"Why, you rat!" said Joanna slowly and softly. "You absolute rat! After all the trouble I've taken. Do you know what I've a good mind to do?"

"You're not going to go and chatter to Annette," Crispin James said smoothly. "That *would* be sawing off your own branch."

"Perhaps. But I should like to have a little conversation with Fair Rosamund and see what she said to it all."

"Her! A lot of use she'd be!" His voice was heavy with scorn. "She knows what I'd do if she started making trouble. She's scared to death as it is. When she found I was back in town she nearly had a heart attack; she knows I could use my influence to have that—that creature put away."

"My dear Cris, what lurid melodrama! And what about

young Hanaker? Suppose I told him a thing or two about his little brother in Paris? You forget I really know quite a lot about you—I could certainly put paid to your chances in the next birthday honours!"

"Look, Joanna," Crispin James said menacingly, "You'll do yourself no good at all by coming here and putting pressure on me like this. You're playing an exceedingly dangerous game and you'd better realise it."

"We'll see about that."

Joanna's voice had suddenly come a lot nearer the door, and on these last words she emerged, walked swiftly across the vestibule, and let herself out. Noel could see that she was trembling with rage. He had just time to flatten himself behind the door before she turned and called back:

"Don't think you've heard the last on this subject. I'll drop in again before I go back to town and see if you've changed your mind."

Crispin James's only reply was to slam the inner door.

Noel allowed Joanna five minutes in which to get clear of the house, and then he softly opened the spring catch of the outer door and followed her into the rainy night.

He had plenty to think about.

There was something very odd in the look that Mrs Kundry gave Annette when she finally answered the door. Annette had thought that by friendliness she was gradually overcoming the little woman's timidity, but now it was back in full strength, compounded with an element of suspicion and—yes, and downright hostility.

"Good evening," Annette said. "I wondered if you would like these? They're some sketches I did of your daughter from memory yesterday."

Mrs Kundry glanced in silence at the sketches as Annette shuffled through the pile, displaying them. She did not comment, nor did she make any move to take them. All of a sudden Annette wondered if she thought they were being offered in unkindness, or mockery?

"I got the idea yesterday that you would have liked a picture of her?" She added hesitantly.

She looked round the bare stone passage in which they stood; there was no furniture save an umbrella-stand. With some diffidence she laid the drawings on this. "I must fly back now—I've got some guests coming in a moment; I was just tidying up when I came across these and wondered if you'd like them. Throw them away if you don't want to keep them."

She smiled at Mrs Kundry and was about to retreat when a smooth voice from behind the little woman said, "Hullo, my dear. And here *is* one of your guests, delayed on the way by a social call."

"Joanna!" Annette said in surprise, reflecting wryly that she must have appeared a considerable fool to Joanna, thrusting her sketches on an obviously unenthusiastic recipient.

"The very same! Just on the point of coming to your door. Well, goodbye, ducky," said Joanna, patting the shoulder of Mrs Kundry, who gave her a watery smile. "I loved our little gossip. Be seeing you again soon."

Beaming, she shepherded Annette out of the house.

"I didn't know you knew Mrs Kundry. You never said, when I mentioned her before," Annette began.

"My dear—the merest acquaintance," Joanna said airily.

"Where's Philip? Isn't he with you?" Annette inquired.

"My dear, we started the evening at this boring cocktail party, and I simply couldn't drag him away. So I seized the opportunity to slip off and pay a couple of *duty* calls. Phil said he'd come straight to your house and skip Mrs K—old ladies are not his *spécialité*."

Annette let Joanna in and offered her a drink.

"Thank you, honey. I've been drinking whisky, so perhaps I'd better stick to that," said Joanna, whose eyes were indeed remarkably bright. "Ouf, your deliciously comfortable chairs, my dear!" And she leaned back with her arms folded, looking so exactly like the cat who has been at the butter that Annette would not have been surprised to hear her start purring. She wondered, pouring the drinks, what Joanna had been up to? She was looking discreetly sophisticated in deep brown with gold earrings, but there was an abnormal tinge of colour in her usually pale cheeks and an almost reckless brilliance in the smile she gave Annette.

"And so I hear it's all fixed up between you and Cris? *Two* proposals in so short a time—my dear, you are a dark horse. Scalps falling like *tenpins!* Darling, I'm so happy for you both, I can't think of two more perfect *soul*-mates. When is the wedding to be?"

"Oh, good gracious." Annette was taken aback, and, though she would hardly admit it to herself, a little hurt; she had not thought Crispin James would tell anybody so soon. But Joanna was his cousin, after all, one must remember. "Not for ages yet, I expect; it's only just decided."

"Oh, but what's to stand in your way?" Joanna said blandly. "Here you are, both of you, adult, free, and rich—or at least, well fixed—so unlike poor working us. If I were you I wouldn't wait to get spliced and *zoom* off to the banks of the Bosphorus, or somewhere blissful and Utopian."

"Oh well—" Annette hedged. "There's lot to be thought about. Anyway, what about you and Philip—why don't you zoom off too?"

"Sweetie, we have to save! We're *church mice!* But seriously, don't you think it would do you a world of good to marry Cris and get away for a long *luxurious* honeymoon?"

"I'd like to go back to the office for a spell first," Annette said stubbornly. "I feel that if I don't do something of my own before—"

"*What?* You're *crazy!*" Joanna's hand jerked and she spilt some whisky. "Go back to work? Oh, you can't mean it!"

"But why not? It's what I've always intended."

"Honey, nobody—but *nobody*—really expects you back. Why don't you just give up the idea and write a nice simple letter of resignation. I'll take it back with me tonight, if you like. Everyone will cry and say, What a *sensible* girl, they'll give you a presentation clock, your conscience will be free, and then, hey for the Dardanelles!"

"But I *want* to go back," Annette's tone was dogged. "It's my life, and I love it. Cris—Crispin won't mind, I'm sure. And I want to see all my friends, Kate and Harris and Tom and Seagram. I feel cut off down here. I—I don't want to get to depend too much on Crispin."

"You can have them for weekends, can't you?"

"It's not the same as working with them."

"But love, anyway you couldn't do that," Joanna said. Without meeting Annette's eyes, she poured herself some more whisky.

"How do you mean?"

"Well—oh hell, I didn't want to have to upset you by telling you this but you'll have to know *sometime* I suppose—they've all left: Kate and Harris and Seagram and Lowinsky; Seagram started being *most* awkward and unreasonable, making mountains out of the most trivial little *molehills*, and in the end—well, in the end things just reached an impasse, after the Rouart business. So he went, and all that little clique of his buddies went with him."

"Went? You mean left? Left the firm?"

"I'm afraid so," Joanna said with careful lightness.

"All my staff? My friends? Then where are they now?"

"I really couldn't say. Seagram talked about going to work for *Vogue*," Joanna said vaguely.

"Did they leave or were they fired?"

"Well, ducky, you know how it is in that sort of complication; decisions are reached by *mutual* agreement."

"You mean you got them sacked!" Annette's eyes were blazing with rage. "You've been secretly working for this all along, haven't you? As soon as I was out of the way you started undermining my position and making things difficult for my staff, and this is the logical outcome. Oh, it's the filthiest thing I've ever heard! And now you've lost the best chief sub and layout man in the firm. Why is this the first I've heard about it? Hadn't I a right to be consulted?"

"Darling, you were ill! I'm sure nobody wanted you worried. Kate—such a *nice* girl, even if she is a bit *dim*—told the others, I believe, that it would not be fair on you to bother you."

"Did you know she was supporting a crippled husband? How will she find another job at her age?"

"I really neither know nor care," said Joanna smoothly. "She wasn't good enough for *that* job, which is all that concerns me. You mustn't let sentiment run away with you, ducky."

"Maybe not," said Annette, standing up and breathing fast. "But I don't need to have you in my house another minute. Perhaps you'll be good enough to tell Philip, if you meet him on the way, that the invitation to dinner is rescinded; he's so adaptable, I'm sure he'll quite understand. Here's your coat. I'm coming back to the office tomorrow if it kills me, and I'll see you there."

"You're a fool, ducky." Joanna shrugged into her coat. She looked half annoyed, half pleased at the way things were working out. "Don't say I didn't warn you, that's all." Her voice was faintly slurred, and her hand at first try missed the doorknob. "Crispin won't be pleased at your change of plan, I can tell you that. It hardly falls in with his own little arrangements."

"Get out!"

With the slam of the door behind Joanna, Annette's rage left her and she suddenly realised that she was completely exhausted; her head felt queerly light, her knees buckled, and the floor turned black-purple and swam up to meet her.

After a lapse of time—how long it had lasted she had no idea—Annette became aware that someone was shaking her shoulder.

"Hullo? I say, are you all right? You look a bit off. Been having a nap? Where's Joanna got to?"

She sat up dazedly and saw Philip squatting before her on the hearth-rug.

"No one seemed to be about," he said, "so I let myself in. I'm afraid I'm rather late—it was one of those parties where everyone talks *so* fast that you can never find a moment to leave. I do apologise."

"It's all right—I must have dozed off." Annette pushed the hair out of her eyes and shook her head to clear it. "Oh my heavens," she said, remembering the quarrel. "Didn't you meet Joanna?"

"Haven't laid eyes on her since she left the Ansons'. She told me she was going to call on some old trout before coming on to you. Why?"

"We had words," said Annette dryly. "I threw her out."

"Oh lord." Philip's expression was just a bit too whimsical to be true. He sat back on his heels, looking like a rueful Greek god. "About the purge? I knew that would come out sooner or later, that you'd be upset."

"Couldn't you do anything to stop her, Philip?"

"Hardly my province, angel. I stick strictly to my camera. And you know what dear Joanna is when she gets the bit between her teeth."

"Well, you'd better go after her now," Annette said as firmly as she could. "I'm sorry about the dinner, but she and I aren't on speaking terms now so I'd better not fraternise—sororise—with you."

"Honey, I'd much rather stay with *you*." Philip gave her one of his charming grins. "To tell you the truth my intended has been as prickly as a prickly pear all day. She didn't like my going off with Everson this morning, and it's been altogether pretty *dread*. She's been hitting the bottle more than somewhat too. I'm beginning to have grave doubts about the whole setup. I can see now that I've been forty different kinds of fool. Annette—I suppose—"

He hesitated, unwontedly for Philip, and gave Annette a curious, almost beseeching look.

"Philip," she said wearily, "I don't know what you're trying to say and I'd much prefer not to guess, but whatever it is, it's better left unsaid. And I think you'd better go now. I've got a bad headache and I shall take some aspirin and get to bed—I'm coming back to London tomorrow."

"Oh—all right. I'm sorry, Annette. Sorry you had a row with Joanna, I mean. I hope it blows over." With less than his customary poise, Philip scrambled to his feet and retreated.

Annette dragged herself up; looking at her shoes, she saw with consternation that they were soaking wet—she must have been out in them, walking in the rain, but when?

Her coat, hanging in the hall, was wet too. She looked at the kitchen clock. It said seven-thirty. Joanna had left before seven. That left over half an hour unaccounted for. What had happened during that time? Where had she been?

Rack her brain as she might, Annette could not remember.

At last she abandoned the fruitless puzzle, pushed it to the back of her mind—with so many other unsolved problems—switched off the lights, and walked slowly and swayingly upstairs to bed.

"Oh, miss! Miss Annette! Wake up! Something terrible's happened!"

Annette rolled over in bed and opened her eyes with a struggle. Her head still ached shatteringly; she pressed her fingers to her forehead.

"What is it, Mrs Fairhall? What's the matter?"

"There, dear, I'm sorry. I didn't know you were still asleep; I didn't mean to startle you. But it's the police—there's an inspector downstairs wanting to see you."

"Police? Why, has there been an accident? Something about the car? What's happened?"

"It's Miss Joanna." The woman's normally pink, cheerful face was white and shocked. "Fairhall found her when he went out to prune the pear tree."

"*Found* her? How do you mean?"

"She's dead, miss. He found her like that."

"*Dead?*"

"Yes, miss. Out there." Mrs Fairhall's eyes wandered to the window, and Annette followed their direction. She pulled on a dressing-gown, went and looked out. A sombre little knot of police stood down at the end of her garden by the rampart wall, huddled together like ravens.

"In my garden? Here? What are they doing?"

"Waiting for ropes to get her down."

Annette looked with mute incomprehension and horror. Mrs Fairhall went on, with equal horror, but also with all the respect due to a thoroughly ghoulish bit of information:

"She's up the pear tree, you see, Miss Annette. Up the pear tree!"

"You mean to say," Annette whispered, "that she *hanged* herself?"

"Oh, no, miss. Kind of perched up in the tree, her body is, as if—well as if somebody had thrown her up there!"

The two women stared at one another with pale, terrified faces.

"Perhaps she's not dead?" Annette suggested. "It—it doesn't seem *possible*."

"Oh yes, she's dead, miss." Mrs Fairhall was positive. "They can tell that from the way she's lying."

"What killed her, then?" Annette was hastily, absently, throwing on some clothes; now she began brushing her hair with quick preoccupied strokes.

"My cousin Jim, he's one of the constables, he did say they reckoned from the look of her neck—but of course can't tell for sure till they get her down—"

"That what?"

"That she'd been strangled, miss."

"*Strangled?*" Annette's eyes met their dark reflections in the mirror; one hand went to her own throat and her mind slowed to a queer semi-paralysis. Strangled! What associations did that word have for her? Rain—a pair of hands clutching a throat—wheels—rain—strangled—

"Rain," she said, and looked out of the window again. It was a fine, clear day, the sky transparent blue. But the grass was wet, littered with the last soaked leaves.

"It was raining last night, wasn't it?" she said, and for the first time wondered if she saw something odd, doubtful, in the anxious look Mrs Fairhall gave her. "When—when do they think it happened?"

"Well, miss, it must have been sometime last night, mustn't it? Oh yes, it was raining. Raining quite heavy from six o'clock on. Miss Joanna came here to dinner last night, didn't she, miss? What time would she have left, then?"

"She didn't stay," Annette said, thinking of the unused dishes and stone-cold food downstairs. "She left early."

There was a knock at the bedroom door. "It's the inspector, miss," said Mrs Fairhall, returning from a colloquy.

"I'll come down," Annette said. "Tell him I'll see him downstairs. Mrs Fairhall—"

"Coffee, duck? I'll get it right away."

"No, not that. But could you—could you ring Mr James and ask if it's convenient for him to come round?"

"Yes, miss. I'll do that right away and then I'll make the coffee."

Annette went down to face the police.

Inspector Curtis was waiting in the dining-room. He was a quiet man, quiet and dark and non-committal; Annette received an intimidating impression of officialdom and reserve and—was it disapproval? Yes, very probably, of interlopers who came from London to live in the peaceful town and involved themselves in such unpleasant affairs. A young uniformed constable stood near the window, very spruce in his dark blue and bright buttons; Annette wondered if he was taking notes but didn't look at him. She kept her eyes waveringly on the inspector's face, and plaited her fingers together.

"This is a most unfortunate affair, Miss Sheldon," the inspector said. "Most unfortunate and mysterious. I believe the young lady was a friend of yours?"

"Well—yes. She was a colleague—an office colleague."

"But you were friendly—you knew her well?"

"Oh yes—yes, very well." Annette took a jerky breath. Too well, she thought. Joanna now lay unrolled before her like a map—all the falsities, the glosses, the calculations.

"I understand she came to dinner with you last night?"

His eyes just brushed the table, with its untouched glass and silver, and returned to Annette.

"She didn't stay," Annette said. "She arrived before dinner and we had a quarrel."

"Indeed?" The voice held no more than mild inquiry, but his eyes were on her alertly.

"It—it was a very bad quarrel." Annette's knuckles were white, now, clenched together. "About office affairs. Miss Southley was running my office for me while I was ill, you understand, and I—and I didn't like the way she was doing it. She had forced a number of my staff to leave."

"Oh yes? By the way, she was engaged to a man who had once been your fiancé, wasn't she?"

"Yes, how did you know that? Yes, she was, but that wasn't what the quarrel was about. It was all over long ago. . . . But after this scene—"

"Yes? What happened then?"

Annette looked about her restlessly. The intense distress she felt was visible only as total pallor; nonetheless a tightening of the atmosphere communicated itself to the inspector. He said again, sharply:

"What happened then?"

She drew a deep breath and said:

"Why, I killed her, Inspector. I strangled her."

"Wait a minute," he interrupted. "You know that anything you say—"

"May be taken down and used in evidence against me? Yes."

"You say you killed Miss Southley. Where did this take place?"

"Outside. In—in the garden."

"Did you know that she had lost an earring? Would you have any objection if we searched for it?"

"Objection?" she said. "Why should I object? Anyway, I can't stop you, can I?"

Having surmounted the immense hurdle of the confession, she was exhausted and apathetic; moving her head, she gave a little twitch to her temples as if they ached painfully and added politely, "I wonder if you'd mind if I took an aspirin, Inspector?"

His eyes were still on her, watchful. He said, "Of course not; I'll get you one," and started towards the door. But before he could reach it, Mrs Fairhall bustled in with a tray of coffee.

She began scolding before she was inside the room.

"Now, you're to leave Miss Sheldon alone, Tom Curtis. She's only just over being very ill, Dr Whitney will tell you the same, and whatever you've been saying to her, I can see it's too much. She's a very delicate young lady and she's not in a fit state to be bothered with questions."

"No," Inspector Curtis said slowly. "No, you're quite right, Mrs Fairhall. I can see she isn't."

Crispin James had been out, but Annette's message brought him striding round to her house when he received it. He found a policeman in her front hall. The house was silent, but full of the dismayed aftermath of a place where something has just happened; it still seemed to echo with shocked, low-voiced discussions and trampling of heavy feet. Annette's brilliant tidiness had been disarranged: newspapers lay strewn, mud and a dead leaf marred the polished floor, a carpet was kicked back.

"I must see Miss Sheldon." Crispin James's tone was peremptory and it came as an anticlimax when the constable politely answered:

"She's in the garden, sir, I believe. Would you like to walk through?"

Annette was on the lawn, looking lost. She wore her brave red coat but it struck a forlorn, garish note against the soaked grass and drooping yellow leaves. Her dark head was bent, and she was strolling aimlessly about. When she saw Crispin James she braced herself with an almost visible effort. He walked up to her quickly and put a hand on her shoulder.

"My dear, this is appalling news. There can't be any mistake? Is she really dead?"

"Oh, *yes*." Her eyes were full of horror. "They've—

they've taken her away. Crispin, she was in—she was in a *tree.*"

He stared at her incredulously, and said as she had done, "She'd hanged herself, do you mean?"

"No, she was lodged in the branches."

"Which tree?" There was still scepticism in his voice.

"That one—the big pear tree."

It was a huge old tree at the foot of the garden, standing against the rampart wall. Originally it had been espaliered, but the upper branches had long since grown away from all control into a dense gnarled mass. A few withered pears still hung on the boughs in the shelter of the immensely thick, thirty-foot wall.

"She was up there," Annette said. Crispin James blankly followed the direction of her pointing finger.

"Up there? In your tree? But how incredible? I didn't really think you meant it." He seemed annoyed, as well as surprised; almost as if he found this a piece of inconsiderate collusion between Annette and Joanna.

After a pause he added, "How did she die?"

"She was strangled." Annette picked up a dead leaf and fiddled with it. "Crispin?"

"Yes, my dear?"

"I have to say a terribly difficult thing. I made a mistake in agreeing to marry you. I've thought it over and I realise that I—I can't. I'm desperately sorry—"

"Annette dear, what nonsense." He took her hands and held them firmly. He was smiling at her, but deep in his eyes was a glimmer of something cold and wary. "You're all upset, and I don't blame you. We won't talk about getting married just at the moment; after all, we've the rest of our lives ahead of us. And this is a most horrible, devastating thing to have happen. But in the course of time it will all be cleared up and forgotten. Look, I brought this for you—"

He pulled out of his pocket a little jewellers' box and opened it. Inside, darkly glinting, was a ring with a huge square-cut ruby the colour of a black-red rose. "See," he said, slipping it on her finger, "isn't it perfect for you?

With your warm ivory skin you should never wear anything but rubies."

"But Crispin—" Unhappily Annette tugged at the ring. Although it had slid on so easily, it refused to budge. "I—I can't. I truly can't. I haven't told you why yet."

"What is it, then, this awe-inspiring reason?"

"I can't ever marry." Annette brought it out flatly. "There's something wrong with me—mentally. I forget things. I have these blackouts."

"Is that all?" His voice was indulgent, relieved. "But, my dear, you know that's only the result of your illness, and being run-down. You didn't have this trouble before you were ill, did you? It will pass, I promise you."

"That's not all," Annette went on doggedly. "It isn't only that sometimes I can't remember what I've been doing. Now I'm beginning to be afraid—afraid that I might find out."

"My dear child, what rubbish have you got into your head? You've been reading too many thrillers. In a few weeks' time when you're completely better you'll find all your memory comes rushing back and then you'll know that you were doing the most simple, harmless things—walking round the ramparts or knitting—"

"I had another blackout last night," Annette said in a low voice. "Joanna and I were quarrelling. I found that behind my back she'd been getting rid of all my staff and I flew into a rage and ordered her out of my house. I meant to pack up some clothes and go up to London this morning by the early train to try and persuade them to come back—"

"What a crazy scheme," muttered Crispin James.

"But instead I came over faint. I—I passed out. Next thing I knew, Philip was there."

"Where was this?"

"In my house."

"Well, there you are. You'd been sitting by the fire all the time. Probably just dropped off to sleep. Quite normal after the shock and upset of a quarrel."

"But Crispin—"

"Well?"

"I hadn't. Because my shoes were wet and so was my coat. Soaking. And I have this horrible half-memory of two hands round a throat—*strangling!* I—I believe I'm a murderer, Crispin. I think I killed Joanna."

"Oh, don't be crazy," he said roughly. But there had been an involuntary pause before he spoke, and the choice of words was not a happy one. Annette, looking up at him, caught his eyes fixed on her in an odd scrutiny—appraisal? Reassessment? "I'm sure you're talking the most absolute, fantastic rubbish," he went on, but his voice had altered almost imperceptibly. "However if I were you I shouldn't mention this notion to anybody—anybody at all—just at this moment. People so quickly get stupid ideas."

"Oh, but I have already."

"How do you mean? Whom have you told?" he said quickly.

"Why, the police. Inspector Curtis. You see it struck me at once," Annette went on, speaking slowly and with difficulty, looking down at her hands while she hopelessly pulled at the heavy ring, "I mean, who would put a body up in a tree but a crazy person—someone who was out of their mind? It's—it's a *mad* thing to do. And anyway, who *could*? Who'd have the strength? But if you're out of your mind—if you go berserk—you have abnormal strength, you can do things that would be quite impossible in the ordinary way. And, really, last night I was so angry that I *could* have killed Joanna."

"Did you tell the inspector this?" Crispin James said, in the same flat, stunned tone.

"Oh yes."

"And what did he say?"

"A policeman wrote it all down and I signed it. About not knowing where I was last night. And he asked me not to leave Crowbridge for the present. So you see, that's why I can't consider marrying you. I'm sorry, Crispin. It wouldn't be fair to you."

"I see." The gentleness of his tone deceived Annette

for a moment. She was aghast to look up at his face and find it so distorted with rage that he seemed like a stranger. "You—*miserable—little—fool!* God in heaven, why does one have to have anything to do with women? Everything that's ever been written about them is true. Can't you see that it's obvious who did it? Why did you have to step in and confuse the issue? God, when I think of the trouble I've taken over you—" In the same soft, deadly voice he began pouring into her ears a stream of savage invective against her, against Joanna, against the inconstancy and hypocrisy and stupidity of all women.

"Don't, Crispin! Oh God, don't! Please don't! I'm sorry, I'm sorry! Oh, please go away!"

She covered her ears, but the abuse still bit through. At last he turned on his heel, furiously grinding a snail-shell into the path as if it gave him intense pleasure to be able to destroy something.

"I'm going down to see Curtis at the police station. Perhaps I'll be able to talk some reason into him," he said over his shoulder. "I'll be back later, and I hope by that time you'll have come to your senses."

"Crispin! Wait! Your ring!"

But the front gate clashed behind him as she was still vainly trying to tug it off. She walked blindly indoors.

"Are you all right, miss?" The policeman in the hall looked at her anxiously. "I was just going back to the station—Mrs Fairhall's out shopping—but I'll wait till she's in if you're feeling bad."

"I'm all right, thanks." In reality she hardly knew what she was doing. *I thought he'd be kind—that he'd understand and help me. Oh, what is going to happen to me?*

At last, faintly, through the fog of despair, she remembered words said to her—could it have been yesterday morning only? It seemed like weeks, months ago: if ever you need any help, will you let me know?

Noel. He was kind, he would not rage at her, nor sear her with abuse. Noel would help her.

She picked up the telephone and got through to the Bell Inn.

"Is Mr Hanaker there? Oh, I see. Out at his site, do you think? Not there—you don't know. I see. Could you ask him to come round and see me as soon as he gets back? Thank you. You don't know when that will be? What about Mr Philip March? He left for London last night? I see. Thank you.

Slowly she replaced the receiver.

VIII

The house felt like a prison. For the first time Annette fully apprehended the fact that Joanna was dead—gay Joanna, spiteful Joanna, lively, false friend. Joanna had told her about this house, persuaded her to come and see it as a therapeutic measure, encouraged her to buy it. And to what end?

Annette looked with horror at the hall and stairs which Mrs Fairhall had now restored to apple-pie order: the old, black banisters, the grape-and-white wallpaper she had chosen with such care. It would be impossible to stay in the house; impossible to paint, sew, read, write. Seeking some escape from the pursuit of her thoughts, she went back into the garden, fetched a broom, and began sweeping dead leaves off the lawn. But she had not been working for more than ten minutes when she became aware that a thin, quiet voice was calling her with the nagging insistence of a metronome.

"Miss Sheldon. Miss Sheldon. Miss Sheldon!"

She saw Mrs Kundry leaning over the dividing hedge.

"Miss Sheldon!" The little woman made a great pantomime of secrecy, screening her hands round her mouth, glancing this way and that. "Would you mind if I spoke to you for a moment?"

Annette nodded and called, "I'll come through. Just a second—"

She hurried back indoors, found a piece of paper and scribbled on it: "Am next door with Mrs Kundry. Shan't be long. Please wait. A."

She underlined the last words and left the paper in the middle of the floor, pinned by a bronze horse, where Noel could not fail to see it if he came round from the Bell. Then she ran back to the garden and made her way along the little path to the house next door.

Annette was feeling so miserable that she was glad of any distraction. She had always wondered vaguely what Mrs Kundry's house would be like inside. Now she received a general impression of age and darkness: old, irregular floors, low ceilings, the dry smell of aged, worm-eaten wood, and a great deal of dust. Through one open door she caught a glimpse of a large loom, and on it a length of a hideous hand-woven material, similar to that of the skirt Mrs Kundry was wearing; then she was led into a gloomy kitchen right at the back of the house. It was bleak and bare, with antiquated equipment of the worst period: grim Victorian range, knobby old gas cooker, oil stove, peeling brown linoleum, chipped stone sink, massive iron mangle.

"I always think the kitchen is the cosiest room of the house, don't you?" chattered Mrs Kundry confidentially. "Sit down while I get you something to eat or a cup of coffee."

Annette demurred, but the thought of coffee was tempting. She had not been able to eat all day, but she had a raging thirst. "Your auntie always used to take a cup with me," said Mrs Kundry reproachfully, seeing her hesitate. "She wasn't a bit proud."

"Miss James, you mean?" Annette obediently sat down.

"Yes, your Auntie Loo."

Annette forbore to correct Mrs Kundry again, but it struck her that the little woman was more than usually distracted and dithering as she pottered about, running a tap, lighting a match, carrying the same article from one point to another and then back again. However, presently she brought Annette a cup of strong, smoky-tasting coffee, poured another for herself, and, sitting down triumphantly at the kitchen table opposite Annette, began sipping, staring over the rim of her cup with bright little beady lashless eyes.

Annette felt ill at ease; the kitchen was so subterranean and dark, with shrubs cutting off what little light came in at the windows; she shivered, and wondered where Doris was—asleep? shut up in some room? The house was intensely quiet.

She had expected that Mrs Kundry wanted to hear all about the police and learn what had been going on, so it was a shock when the little woman suddenly remarked:

"You're not very happy in this town, are you?"

"Well—" Annette began. She hardly knew what to reply.

"Mind, I don't blame you. It's a funny little old hole, quiet. The people are a queer lot. I don't have much to do with them these days, though I was a Crowbridge girl. I've lived in this house for years; it was my mother's. Ever since she died I've been here. Of course I've been abroad too, I know what foreign ways are like. But the people here—they're inbred. It's not a good thing, that, you know. It makes them queer."

"Really?" said Annette vaguely, drinking her strong coffee.

"Do you know," Mrs Kundry leaned forward confidentially, "do *you* know, some of the families go right back to Roman days?"

"Oh, but surely—"

"They do! Mine for one." Her eyes shone with triumph. "My mother used to have papers proving it—all lost now, of course. Lost, burnt, mislaid . . ." Mrs Kundry looked absently about her as if she had also mislaid the thread of what she was saying, then recalled it and added with a knowing nod, "What's more, I'm the reincarnation of a Roman priestess."

"Goodness, how—how very interesting." Annette felt this was not the proper response. Mrs Kundry was behaving more and more oddly; could Crispin James have been right when he said that she was not quite sane? Annette was beginning to feel uneasy about her hostess.

"And Doris," Mrs Kundry continued, leaning forward still further and speaking in a low tone, "Doris is my oracle! That's why I have to see that they never take her away." She gave Annette a conspiratorial smile. Annette could think of no response but to nod and smile back; she found all of a sudden that she was excessively tired, almost incapable of coherent thought.

"Of course your auntie played me a very bad turn," Mrs Kundry said unexpectedly and irrelevantly. "Coming here, drinking my coffee, giving me to understand I'd receive something handsome in her will, and then what does she do? Leaves it all to a cats' home. Oh she was a deep one, she was. But mind you I bear no malice, none. Though your family has done me two cruel wrongs, I'm not one to brood over my injuries."

"I think you're confusing me with Joanna," Annette began cautiously, and then she was visited by a new and terrifying possibility as to the authorship of Joanna's death. She looked uneasily at Mrs Kundry—but she felt so tired, and the occasion was so dreamlike, that she could not formulate her thought into a question.

"But that isn't what I brought you here to tell you," Mrs Kundry went on. "No, it was about Crispin. He's asked you to marry him, hasn't he?"

"I don't see that it's any business of yours. Nor can I think who told you." But then Annette remembered Joanna's call on Mrs Kundry yesterday. "However, I'm not going to marry him, as it happens. I've told him I can't."

"You've told him you can't, have you?" Mrs Kundry began to laugh quietly to herself. "Oh, that's funny, that is! Then why—" she suddenly reached out across the table and took Annette's hand, "Why are you wearing that ring? And why were you kissing him the other night? I saw you, I was out in the garden picking a few herbs, and I saw he'd put the charm over you just the way he has over plenty of other people. Not over me, though! Not over me any more! I'm protected against him now!"

"Mrs Kundry," Annette said quickly, "I think I'd better be getting back to my own house. You really haven't any right to say these things to me, and let me assure you I am *not* going to marry Crispin James."

She tried to stand up, but found to her dismay that her head was swimming. She subsided groggily onto her chair again.

"No, I should think you're not!" Mrs Kundry was smiling, but her eyes were watchful. "One reason being that he's married already. Why, whose daughter is Doris, do you suppose?"

"No! I don't believe it!"

But already, as the incredulous words left her, Annette realised, even through her stupor of fatigue, that it was Crispin of whom Doris had reminded her—the likeness between their faces was unmistakable, once you knew. *That* was why he hated seeing her, that was why he hated any evidence of mental instability—because she was his own child! That was why he had been so angry. It all hung, horribly, together.

"Oh yes, he married me." Mrs Kundry stood up and began walking about, picking things up, shaking them, and putting them down in the oddest way while she threw out a series of remarks, keeping her lashless eyes fixed all the time on Annette's face.

"He didn't want to get married a bit, but he had to, you see. Doris was on the way. Besides, twenty years ago I was pretty enough. I used to sit for him then. *And* I had a bit of money. That was how I got to know him, posing. But when my mother found out, she put a stop to it, she gave away a picture he did of me. So then he went abroad and I followed, and we got married. I didn't tell my mother; she'd have stopped the money. I wrote and told her I'd married an Austrian; I called myself Kundry. Crispin soon got through the money, anyway, and I couldn't paint, I was no use to him that way. When Doris came, that was the end. He couldn't stand the sight of her as soon as she began to grow—you know. Told me I'd got to have her put in a home. As if I'd ever do such a terrible thing! Why she's all I have. Then he left me. Went to Mexico and wrote and said he'd divorced me. Mexico! I knew it was a lie. I wasn't in Mexico, was I? I'm still your wife, I told him. But when my mother died I came back to Crowbridge and put it round that my husband had died. Crispin was angry, I can tell you, when he heard I was back here; he didn't like it, but there wasn't much he could do. And he was mostly abroad. But he said that if it ever came out that Doris was his, he'd see she was put away. The wicked, cruel brute! Oh, he's a schemer, that one! Doris has always been a comfort to me, she's a good girl to her mother. So I've been careful. Nobody knows except Miss James and she's promised not to tell. *Why don't you give me my ring?"*

The sudden intensity of the last words took Annette by surprise. Before she could muster her wits, Mrs Kundry had tugged at the ring and, by knack or good fortune, got it off.

"That's better," she said, slipping it on her own finger. "Of course, there were others he took up with after me, but I'm his *legal* wife; he did have some poor girl in Munich who jumped out of a window. He gets fed up with people, you know: picks their brains, milks them dry, and then that's the finish. But not me, oh no! I may be quiet, and I'm scared of him, but I'm *waiting;* I've got my own resources."

"But couldn't you—didn't you have any claim on him for support?" Annette said with a dazed stab at practicality through the mist of nightmare.

"And have him get Doris put away? Not me. Your Auntie Loo tried to make me go to court but I was too scared. I said I'd wait till Doris was a big girl, big enough to be a help to her poor mother. *Do you know who I believe you are?"* said Mrs Kundry, staring at Annette with bright-eyed intensity. "I believe you're Louisa James come back again. With all your money. You've got a lot more now, haven't you? And this time you won't leave it to a cats' home, will you? This time you're going to leave it to me as you ought. And Crispin won't see a penny of it."

"Mrs Kundry—I—I don't think you're well." Annette got the words out with difficulty. Her tongue lay limp in her mouth and almost refused to form the words. "You're saying a lot of things that aren't true. I'll go home now—we'll forget all this."

But how could she forget it? Through the improbabilities, the crazy exaggerations, was there not visible a skeleton of truth?

"Oh no, you can't go home, dear," Mrs Kundry said reprovingly. "You just sit quietly there a bit longer. I've given you one of Doris's pills; you'll find you're quite comfy, but just a little bit sluggish."

"But I must go back! The police asked me to stay in my own house."

"Police? What have they got to do with it?" said Mrs Kundry, busily hunting about in a drawer full of string, bottle-tops, and miscellaneous oddments. "Where did I put that Bible? I just want you to promise that I'll get all the money that's my right this time—perhaps we'd better have it in writing too—and *then* you can go back to the place from whence you came. Poor dear, you must be so tired. But at least it isn't far to the churchyard. And you'll sleep better with an easy conscience."

The doorbell rang.

"What a nuisance. Who can that be?" Mrs Kundry looked nervously startled and annoyed. "We certainly don't want them interrupting us, do we? *I* know. I'll just pop you in Doris's wheel-chair behind the curtain here—"

She pulled back a hessian curtain across an alcove which had probably once contained a boiler, and disclosed Doris's wheel-chair.

At the sight of it, shock and the relaxing drug she had been given suddenly combined to open the doors of memory in Annette's mind. Clearly and completely she remembered driving home across Crowbridge marshes, the lift she had given Mrs Kundry and Doris, the strangling hands on her throat. Of course! That was what she had forgotten. Then perhaps Doris—perhaps Joanna's death—? After Joanna had left, that night—

"Where—where's Doris?" she tried to articulate.

"Quite safe, quite safe, upstairs," chattered Mrs Kundry,

busily manoeuvring the chair into position beside Annette. "There, dear, we'll just tuck you in like that." With a totally unexpected strength—but of course she was used to lifting Doris about—she manhandled Annette into the wheel-chair. Annette, strangely placid and obedient in her drugged state, let herself be shifted like a doll. "That's it, dear. Now we'll just run you in behind the curtain and there you'll be, quite safe and sound. Don't speak, will you dear?"

The curtain fell in front of Annette. Through its loose sacklike weave she could still vaguely distinguish objects, and could hear quite clearly; she could identify the voices of Mrs Kundry and Crispin James coming nearer down the passage and heard him say as he came into the room:

"I tell you, she must be here somewhere. Here's her note. Where is she? Where is Miss Sheldon?"

"I—I'm not sure of the name!" Mrs Kundry's voice was twittering with terror; she kept as far from Crispin James as she could. "Go away, go away, Crispin! I—I'm not frightened of you. You leave me alone. I don't bother you, so don't you bother me."

"You don't bother me?" he said savagely. "What about bringing your abomination down to the bazaar in full view of everyone? What sort of behavior do you call that? Do anything else of the kind and I'll have her put away, as she ought to have been years ago."

"Oh no, Crispin, no, please! I'm no trouble to you. I don't ask you for money. And no one in the town knows there's any connection between us except Louisa James, and she ought to have been dead months ago, poor soul. I've never asked you for anything, have I, since you left me in Hamburg."

"You wouldn't get any money if you did ask for it," he said sourly. "Come on, tell me where Annette Sheldon is, I found this note in her house, so I know she's here."

"Why do you want her?"

"My good Rosamund, it's none of your business, but if you must know she's my student, a talented painter, and I'm interested in seeing that she comes to no harm."

"Oh, yes, she's one of those, isn't she?" Mrs Kundry sounded more rational; she seemed to be pulling herself together. "It's that as well as her money you're after. You're going to put the spell on her to paint your pictures, are you—like poor Hilde in Munich and the boy in Paris and the others?" Mrs Kundry gave a nervous high-pitched giggle. "Poor Crispin! It must be terrible for a painter to run out of ideas for pictures. It's lucky you find these young helpers, isn't it? Not so lucky for them, of course. How did you get rid of the boy in Paris? Tell him to drink his nice cocoa when the clock struck twelve and leave a dose of rat-poison in it? That's such a clever way of yours. It didn't work with me, did it? You couldn't get me to do things that way."

"Oh, shut up, Rosamund! For the last time, where is Annette? Do I have to search the house for her? I'm at the end of my patience, I warn you. Joanna found it dangerous to meddle with me; I had to deal with her; do you want to follow her?"

"Oh, no, Crispin, please! I think your girl must have slipped in when my back was turned, perhaps she's upstairs; I'll look, I'll hunt, I promise—" Mrs Kundry sounded terrified again. She pattered out of the kitchen, muttering to herself, and Annette heard her go upstairs.

"Hurry up!" Crispin James shouted after her. "Annette! Are you up there?"

Doors opened and shut somewhere in the house, boards creaked, it seemed as if furniture were being moved about. There was a thumping on the stairs.

"What the devil are you doing?" Crispin James called impatiently.

There followed a pause, and then a lot of things happened one on top of the other.

Mrs Kundry's voice could be heard outside the door crying gleefully, "Go on, Doris, that's him, that's your father! The one I've told you about! The man who left us high and dry in Hamburg. Go on, you're a big girl now. We made a mistake that day in the castle, it wasn't him, but this time it really is; this is the day we've been waiting for. Go on, Doris, you're big enough to do what I taught you. Now you'll see, Crispin! Now you'll see that you can't bully people and get away with it forever. You can frighten me, but you can't frighten *her!*"

Mrs Kundry's voice rose to a triumphant shriek of hate. Doris apparently charged into the room: Annette heard a crash as a chair fell over, and the hoarse breathy voice that she remembered from that earlier time in the car: *"Now I've got you! I've waited a long time for this! Now I've got you!"*

"Get away from me, you harpy!" shouted Crispin James.

This was succeeded by sounds of frantic, confused scuffling—gasps, a sudden sharp cry of pain, thuds of furniture being overturned, a choked exclamation from Crispin James—"Take your hands off my throat, damn you!"—and then a loud crash and the clatter of fire-irons.

There came a shriek from Mrs Kundry. "Oh! You've hurt her! You've killed her!"

"Shut up!" said Crispin James softly and fiercely. "She's only stunned. Do you want the whole street to know your daughter's a homicidal maniac?"

"She's dead, she's dead, I tell you. You killed her with the poker."

"Rubbish! Chuck some water on her and she'll come to. Not in here, though—I'm not having her hands round my throat again. *You* taught her to do that, you devil—"

"What if I did? How about the way *you* treated *me?*"

"For heaven's sake stop that noise or I won't help you," snapped Crispin James. "Here, carry her upstairs—take her head—*Quiet,* there are police next door as it is—"

There was a slow shuffling, which gradually died away up the stairs. Presently Annette heard Crispin James's step returning.

She summoned what seemed enough energy to push over the Albert Memorial, and just managed to achieve a faint croak:

"Crispin!"

There was a pause. Then Crispin's voice came, guardedly, full of astonishment, "*Annette!* Is that you?"

"I'm—I'm—" she tried to say, "I'm behind the curtain," but the effort was too great. "I'm here."

Quick steps approached. The hessian was snatched aside.

"Annette! Good God, it *is* you! Why didn't you say you were there before?" He looked horribly startled. He was smoothing his disordered grey hair, setting straight a tie pulled wildly askew.

"I can't—couldn't—" She made a weak gesture with one hand. "Take me away—please—"

He looked at her sharply. "Did Mrs Kundry give you something? A drug?" His eyes fell on the coffee cups.

Annette nodded. The slowed-up processes of her mind had begun gently moving again. Where were Mrs Kundry and Doris? They were very quiet. Doris had been hurt—she had attacked Crispin James, who was her father. Mrs Kundry was upstairs with her. What was that remark Mrs Kundry had made? "You put the spell on her to paint your pictures for you . . ." Somehow, out of the ugliness and violence of the episode that has passed, this alone stayed in Annette's mind. Do I paint my own pictures or Crispin's, she wondered.

Crispin James pulled a handful of objects out of his pocket and from them picked out a lens. Through it he looked intently into the pupil of Annette's eye.

"How much can you remember?" he asked insistently.

"You hurt Doris."

"Well, good God, girl, don't you realise how she came at me? The old hag must have been training her for years past—if ever there was a case of self-defense that was it—what are you looking at?"

"That's"—Annette stretched her hand waveringly towards the matches and other oddments from Crispin's pocket on the table—"that's Joanna's gold earring. The police were looking for it in my garden and all over the house too. One of them was missing. *You* had it. Why was it in your pocket?"

Her slow, wandering gaze travelled up to his face. His lips were pressed together, his eyes dark and unreadable.

"You said Joanna found it was dangerous to meddle with you. You said you had to deal with her. Did *you* kill Joanna?"

"Why in the world should I do such a thing?" But his expression was watchful, hostile. "Tell me," he said, putting his face close to hers and speaking very clearly, "did you hear everything Rosamund and I were saying?"

"Oh yes." Annette's tone was dreamy. "She is married to you and Doris is your daughter—Doris is very like you I see now—and you put spells on people—some boy in Paris—was he Noel's brother? And a girl in Munich. Did you put a spell on me too? To make me paint your pictures?"

"Hell and damnation," said Crispin James. He stared at Annette sombrely. "Your wits are altogether too sharp, my dear. I suppose if I were to get you away from here, your Puritan conscience would take you straight to the police? Would it? Would you tell the police about Joanna's earring? And what I said?"

"Oh yes, I'll have to," Annette said with drug-induced simplicity.

He stared at her dangerously. "I forbid it! Do you understand?" Picking up a pencil, he tapped three times on the table. His eyes bored into hers. "You are going to sleep. You will forget this whole scene. Your eyes are closing. I order you to go to sleep."

But Annette was not going to sleep. The drug she had taken, plus her shocked state, combined against him. She pulled herself back in her chair, forcing herself to look at him calmly. "I—I believe you are a murderer, Crispin. I believe you murdered Joanna," she said with slow, careful articulation.

He stood staring at her a moment longer, indecisive, savage in disappointment, like a child who has accidentally broken his toy.

"If you feel that way, then there's only one thing to be done, isn't there? This house is due to burn down shortly, and I'm afraid you'll have to go with it. I'm sorry to kill the goose that lays the golden eggs, my dear—*very* sorry

I've had all this work for such a small reward—but I must cut my losses. Luckily the world is full of dear little geese. And at least I have some of the eggs."

He looked into her eye through the lens again.

"You won't be stirring yet awhile. However. I'll lock the door to be on the safe side. Don't worry about Rosamund—she's snug upstairs, locked in too. And if Doris should come round and wander down—well, people may believe she started the fire . . ." Deliberately he walked round the room wiping possible fingerprints off anything he might have touched and then, using a handkerchief, overturned the oil heater against the hessian curtain and put a match to it, sprinkling the rest of the oil about the room.

"A few more chairs overturned—Joanna's earring can stay, it will be useful corroborative evidence that she was murdered by Doris—or by you, perhaps?—a nice puzzle for the police—and I think, yes, I think the gas on. That's all. Even should you have the energy to call for help, which I very much doubt, there will hardly be time. Or anyone to hear. Goodbye, my love."

He leaned over and kissed her. Annette, with her last shred of strength, raised her hand and brought its nails down his cheek, tearing five red and bleeding weals.

"You little vixen!" he muttered, starting back. At that moment a breath of wind blew the flame from the curtain, which was now burning fiercely, to a heap of crumpled paper against the wall. A fan of flame leapt upwards and Crispin James retreated quickly to the door. The lock clicked.

Annette sat placidly watching the fire. Her mind took in the impact of the things that were happening, the fact that she was in deadly danger—but her body had shot its bolt and refused to do any more. Relaxed and peaceful she sat watching the flames until one of them actually licked at her hand; then she did get up and take a staggering step towards the back door.

IX

"Thank you, Mr Hanaker," Inspector Curtis said. "Those letters from your brother to Mr James are very interesting, no doubt—'Sometimes I think that if you told me to go and jump in the Seine I shouldn't be able to help doing it'— but they don't exactly amount to proof of anything, do they? And I'd very much like to know how you got hold of them. I assume Mr James didn't give them to you."

"No, he didn't exactly."

"And I still don't quite see why you are here."

"Because I've had enough of Crispin James and his murky goings-on," Noel said violently. "As far as I can gather he's now planting Joanna Southley's murder on to Ann—on to Miss Sheldon."

Inspector Curtis said calmly, "There has never been any question of that. We discounted Miss Sheldon's self-accusation completely, both from your story and from Dr Whitney's report on her. In any case what Mr James said to us was that Mrs Kundry's half-witted daughter was probably responsible. We know now that Joanna Southley was strangled first, elsewhere, and that her body was carried along the ramparts and thrown down into Miss Sheldon's garden, where it lodged in the pear tree."

"Well, there you are!" Noel said. "Crispin James's studio has a flight of steps that leads up onto the rampart. It would have been easy enough for him to carry her along, and he probably intended to drop her in Mrs Kundry's garden. He could have made a mistake, that dark night. I daresay she went back to his studio to tell him that she had quarrelled with Miss Sheldon, and that Miss Sheldon was planning to go back to London. She would want that prevented somehow, and Crispin was the only person who *could* prevent it."

"All this is highly far-fetched," the inspector said dubiously. "If he had threatened her, it would have been foolhardy to go back."

"She was an extremely self-confident person. She probably didn't take the threat seriously."

"There are other possibilities though," Inspector Curtis pointed out coldly. "Mr March, for instance. Why did he leave so suddenly? Two men are going round to his London address. The feeble-minded girl is another possibility, though we've never had any complaints about her before—I always understood she was paralysed. We might be a step further if we could find Joanna Southley's missing earring. It's nowhere in the garden or on the ramparts."

"Search me if you want," Noel said.

"That's all right, Mr Hanaker, you're in the clear as far as time of death goes. We haven't any suspicions directed at you. But all you've told me doesn't quite add up to a motive for Crispin James, does it?"

"I haven't finished yet," Noel said. "As I've told you, half the paintings in Crispin James's studio with his signature on them are not by him at all but by his pupils, painted in a state of hypnotic trance. Don't you think a man might be willing to commit murder to prevent a damaging fact like that from coming out?"

"But this is all hearsay—not the sort of evidence we could produce in a court of law. How can you prove any of it? Nobody's been present at one of his lessons."

"No, but I know people in Paris who can describe my brother during the last months of his life—his behaviour was very typical."

"And the pictures," Curtis went on sceptically, "how can you prove they are not by James himself?"

"I know my brother's work. I could swear to it—even when it's coerced into an imitation of James's style. He had some very characteristic brush tricks."

"*You* know, perhaps, sir, but who else?"

"Well, if you don't think that's a line," said Noel doggedly, "listen to this tape-recording."

He planted the box he had brought with him on the inspector's desk, opened it, and flicked a switch. The tape began to turn.

Inspector Curtis stared at him, half scandalised, half fascinated.

"You're fairly familiar with Crispin James's voice and intonation?" Noel said. "You'll have it in mind if he's recently been in here—do you recognise that?"

. . . "Sit down in the cane chair and rest a minute," the harsh voice said . . . "we mustn't forget that you are still a convalescent."

They heard Annette's laugh and some talk, evidently relating to a picture, Crispin James giving technical instructions about reflections. Annette's replies became slower and more sleepy, presently stopped altogether. Then Crispin James's voice came through alone:

"Your eyes are growing heavier and heavier. They are shut. You are asleep."

Noel's eyes met those of the inspector.

"Annette," the voice said. "Can you hear me? Do you know who I am?"

"Yes," she said faintly.

"Good. Now I am going to tap three times on the easel with the handle of this brush."

Tap. Tap. Tap.

"Can you hear that?"

"Yes."

"From now on, whenever you hear me tap three times like that, whatever you may be doing, you will fall into a deep sleep immediately. Do you understand? You will not fall asleep if you hear anybody else tap. But whenever I tap three times—like this—you will go to sleep. And when you are asleep, mine are the only orders you will obey, and you will do whatever I tell you. You will paint pictures—and you will paint them for me. Do you understand?"

"Yes," she said.

"What do you want to paint now?"

"A view of the marsh," she said drowsily.

"Very well. You may start tomorrow. But it shall be as I direct. Now, I am going to count downwards from six, and when I reach one you will wake up. Consciously, you will remember nothing of what I have told you. Now you will start to wake. Six—five—four—lighter and lighter—three—two—waking up—one. You're wide awake."

"Now do you see?" said Noel. He switched off the tape. "There are lots more like that—dozens. She went there so often that it was all too easy to nip in and plant tapes at likely times."

"But that was highly illegal!" the inspector said, shocked. "We couldn't possibly admit evidence taken in such a way. Besides, in any case, I don't know that a tape-recording would be—"

Such things evidently came outside his professional experience.

"But you admit that's Crispin James's voice? And Miss Sheldon's?"

"Well," the inspector said dubiously, "it *sounds* like them. But there again we'd have to get expert opinion. And if he denied it, as he'd be sure to—"

"All right, well, wait a minute before we begin to argue. Listen to this last one. It's a bit blurred because I took it more or less through a keyhole."

He slipped out the tape and put in another, flicked the switch.

Crispin James's voice came again:

"Well, what's this important thing you've dragged me away from the Ansons' to tell me?"

"This was taken last night," Noel murmured. Inspector Curtis gave a faint nod of acknowledgment. He was listening intently. The tape spun on.

. . . "You're playing an exceedingly dangerous game and you'd better realise it."

"We'll see about that." Joanna's voice suddenly increased in volume. "Don't think you've heard the last on this subject. I'll drop in again before I go back to town and see if you've changed your mind."

A door slammed.

Noel clicked the tape off.

"Now, have you got a motive there?" he asked after a moment.

Inspector Curtis was looking dazed.

"Of course we couldn't use the tape as evidence," he muttered, "but it might form a basis for questioning. It's unfortunate that Miss Sheldon suffers from this amnesia. We can hardly question her any more—"

"Hell," Noel said angrily. "It's more than amnesia! It's the result of being in constant deep hypnosis. Soon she'll hardly be in our world at all. If you won't do something, *I* will. That girl has got to be rescued before things get any worse. I came to England to get a fix on Crispin James because of what he did to my brother—my sister and I were convinced all along that he was at the bottom of Rob's extraordinary disintegration—and this gives me my chance; this time James has really done himself. I'm going round to Annette Sheldon's house now. I'll leave the tapes with you."

"Remember, sir, she's not strong. If she's given any kind of shock—"

"You're telling me?" said Noel, and was gone.

Inspector Curtis, looking as if he expected it to bite him, switched the tape-recorder on again.

Dusk was falling when Noel rang Annette's bell. Mrs Fairhall answered it.

"Mr Hanaker!" she said in astonishment. "Do you know where Miss Sheldon's got to? I thought she must be with you. She's not at Mr James's, I know. Someone from that London office has been on the phone, urgent. Her coat's here, the one she usually wears—I can't think where she can be—"

A knot of fear formed in Noel's stomach.

"She isn't in the garden?"

"She didn't answer when I called. I was just going to take another look in case she'd come over queer—"

Noel walked through the house, Mrs Fairhall anxiously following, and made his way down the lawn to the end of the garden. Without confiding his fears to Mrs Fairhall, he stared up into the pear tree and searched among the bamboo clumps. But Annette was nowhere to be seen.

"You don't think she had one of her come-overs, sir?" Mrs Fairhall said fearfully. "And—and perhaps made away with herself?"

"She's been in a lot of emotional tension," Noel said. "You're sure she's not with Mr James, though?"

"No, sir. She had a quarrel with him and he went off in a huff. He came back later looking for her but she'd gone by then."

They turned back towards the house. Mrs Fairhall exclaimed:

"Mercy gracious, look at that blaze! Whatever can they be burning in Mrs Kundry's house?"

Clouds of smoke were billowing out of the downstairs windows next door, and a dim and flickering light was beginning to show behind the kitchen windows.

"Cripes!" said Noel. "That's more than burnt toast." He broke into a run, calling back over his shoulder, "Better ring the fire-brigade, Mrs F."

Threading the little path through Mrs Kundry's overgrown garden, he reached the back door and banged on it. No one answered. The door was locked.

"Are they all out?" he thought. "Or deaf? Or dead?"

He remembered that Annette had said there was something queer about her neighbour; but surely queerness would not extend to ignoring a blaze on this scale? He banged again and shouted, "Hey! Hey there! Anybody in?"

The door resisted him. At last he put his foot on the lock and broke it open. The room beyond was a choking welter of flame-threaded smoke, through which a blackened figure came staggering. It was not until she was close beside him that he recognised Annette.

"Upstairs!" she coughed. "Mrs Kundry and Doris, upstairs!"

Then she collapsed against him.

The police and the fire-brigade arrived simultaneously five minutes later. Noel, having left Annette with Mrs Fairhall, was trying to fight the flames with a garden hose in order to get up the stairs, which by this time were a roaring tunnel of fire. The house was old, and much of it matchboard-panelled; before long the blaze was hopelessly out of control. The kitchen, where it had started, was like a furnace—impossible to enter.

"There are two women upstairs!" Noel shouted to Inspector Curtis, who presently appeared in the smoke near him.

"Not any more," the inspector said. "The firemen got them out of the first-floor windows just before the fire reached there. I came to get *you* out."

"Are they all right?"

"One of them is—the other one's had her head bashed in. When did you get here, sir?"

"I came straight here from you," Noel said. "Miss Sheldon wasn't at home. Then we saw the fire. Miss Sheldon's got a story for you: Crispin James was here. Mrs Kundry's daughter went for him and he set fire to the place. Now will you believe me when I say he's a dangerous killer? You'd better get after him fast before he decamps; even he can hardly be expected to face this out."

The inspector cogitated for a moment, then, coming to a quick decision, ran out to his car, summoning a couple of constables.

"I'm coming too!" Noel shouted, and threw himself into the car with them. It lurched over the cobbles towards Benedict Street.

Nobody answered when they rang Crispin James's bell. They went up the outside steps to the studio. Curtis rapped on the door, which was half open as usual, and went in. Crispin James was in the studio, working at the easel with his back to the door.

"Go away," he called without turning. "I'm busy finishing a picture. I can't be disturbed."

"Sorry sir; this is police business."

"I tell you, I'm busy," Crispin James said petulantly. "Make an appointment with my man downstairs."

Rage in Noel had been building up to a crescendo. "Turn round, can't you, and face up to it!" he burst out furiously. But Crispin James merely hunched his shoulders, sinking his neck between them, and scraped ostentatiously at his palette with a knife. He said without turning round:

"I wish you could understand that I'm a man of considerable importance—a genius! Will you all please go away? I should *not* be disturbed in this manner."

Noel, quite beside himself, sprang forward and grabbed Crispin James's shoulder to spin him round. The face that James turned was a shock to them—it was dead white, covered with sweat, and marred by five angry weals down one cheek. His hair was rumpled, there were smudges of dust on his shirt-front.

"I'm afraid, sir, I must ask you to explain—" Curtis began.

"Oh, leave me alone, can't you leave me alone? Isn't it possible for you to realize that I'm busy with highly important work?" Crispin James's tone was somewhere between a snarl and a whine. Noel was flabbergasted at the way in which he had aged in the last few hours: he was stooped, his cheeks had fallen in, his dark eyes had lost their curious luminosity. Even his magnificent mane of frosty hair seemed to have dulled and yellowed.

"I'm afraid your work must wait. We wish to ask you some questions regarding the recent fire at the house of Mrs Kundry, number four, Crossbow Lane. Mrs Kundry said—*Stop him!*"

Jabbering angrily to himself about blasted interlopers, Crispin James had snatched up a long thin blade like a kitchen knife and thrust his way past the two constables.

Taken by surprise, they gave way before him. Noel tackled him and got a slash on his hands; Curtis leapt for the door, grabbing a wood mallet, and got there first. Crispin James hesitated; the constables had recovered and while one guarded the lobby door the other, with Noel, began closing in.

Crispin James gave a quick, hunted glance round the room. Noel made a dart for him, but with the speed of a lizard he dodged away sideways and made for the open window. There he turned, trembling, and screamed at them, "Hell and damnation, you fools, why can't you leave me in peace?" then launched himself into mid air.

Noel and the two policemen stood rooted with horror. Curtis, after a moment, went gingerly to the window and peered out down the twenty-foot drop and came back rather pale.

"Not the way I'd choose to die," he said briefly. "But at least it was quick. Quicker than he deserved, probably."

Noel was not listening. He had already left the big room with its piles of paintings and was running down the stairs, out of the gate, along the street to Annette's house.

She was in hospital a fortnight. The second time Noel came to see her he brought her a bunch of holly and Christmas roses.

"Compliments of the season," he said cautiously. Annette smiled at him.

Spondee planted his large feet on the pillow, shook his dusty ears, and gave her a melting look while he beat the counterpane with his tail.

"Have you noticed," Noel said, "he wags his tail in trochaic measure."

"What nonsense you talk. And I'm sure dogs aren't allowed in hospital," Annette said.

"Dogs? You call that thing a dog? He's an anachronism."

"Oh, well, that's all right then. The hospital's full of those; they hardly seem to know the difference between a bed-pan and a warming-pan."

"Yow!"

"Noel," Annette said presently, "I wanted to ask you

before but I felt too weak—how did you come to go to the police?"

"Well," he said, "I'd been keeping an eye on Crispin James because I was dead set on getting some proof of what he'd done to Rob. And perhaps stopping him from doing it to anybody else. When I talked to you the night Joanna was killed—"

"To me?"

"Yes, don't you remember? You rang up, all in a stew because you'd quarrelled with her, and asked me to take you for a walk. We went along to the Bell and had coffee—sitting full in the public eye right through the time when Joanna was being done in—and you told me you'd started to feel unhappy about your painting lessons. It was then that I decided to go to the police next day. Had you forgotten that?"

"I had," Annette said, smiling at him with a brilliant sunrise face, "but now I do remember. Then you brought me home and told me to take off my wet things and kissed me good night."

"Forward of me, wasn't it?" said Noel grinning.

"I must have sat down in the armchair and gone straight off to sleep. And next day I'd forgotten all about it and thought I'd been out murdering Joanna. But of course Crispin did that," she added, recollecting. "He as good as said so. And he had her earring."

"She'd threatened to show him up, you see."

"How could I have been so gullible?" Annette said, half to herself. "Now it all seems like some queer, twisted dream."

"He had a tremendously powerful personality; you weren't by any means the only one. It was astonishing how he put it over on all sorts of people. But as soon as one saw through him it stuck out a mile; I used to wonder how on earth you succeeded in *not* seeing him for the horrible old phony he was. All that line of talk!

"But he was a good painter once," Annette said sadly. "Let's not talk about him."

"No, let's not."

He had never asked how much she remembered of her lessons; never would. Such recollections were best left undisturbed to die a natural death.

"By the way, where *did* Philip get to?"

"He just decided that Joanna was too much of a handful and bunked back to London. He didn't even know she was dead till the police told him."

"I've had a letter from the office; they've given me convalescent leave for another six months, then they want me to go back if I possibly can. They've got someone temporary for now. It sounds as if they really want me. But I'm not quite sure what to do in the meantime. I shan't stay here—I'm going to sell my house. I can't stand the thought of it."

"That makes my task easier then," Noel said cheerfully. "Inspector Curtis asked me to break it to you gently when I thought fit: your house, along with Mrs Kundry's, was burned down to its foundations—the fire had got too strong a hold to stop it."

"Burned? My house? Right down?" Her dark eyes were enormous in her thin face.

"I'm afraid so. Are you very upset?"

"I'm delighted," she said flatly. "I could never have lived in it again."

"Good-oh. That brings me to my next point," he went on, looking at her cautiously. "Listen, didn't Dr Whitney suggest you should go on a cruise before you started work again?"

"Ye-es, he did, but cruises always sound so idle-rich and revolting; I'm sure I couldn't stand the other passengers."

"Well, I have an invitation for you. From my mother. To stay on a small farm near Mount Ruapehu. There's just her and Jill, my sister, and Father. Would you like that?"

"Noel, I'd love it! Have they really invited me? How wonderful of them. I'd like to meet them so much. Goodness, New Zealand! Do you sail or fly?"

"It takes two months if you sail. Nice time to put you

back on your feet. And if you sail, I'm coming too. I'm not forgetting that you said a while back that we hardly know one another. Roman remains can wait. After all," Noel said largely, "Roman remains are common enough, but the chance of getting to know you on a two-month trip comes only once in a lifetime. We can take it nice and slow, like this."

He kissed her again, suiting the action to the adverb.

Spondee's smile reached his ears, and his tail accelerated into a series of regular anapaests.

www.ingramcontent.com/pod-product-compliance
Ingram Content Group UK Ltd.
Pitfield, Milton Keynes, MK11 3LW, UK
UKHW022309280225
455674UK00004B/236